IZZY NEWTON AND THE S.M.A.R.T. SQUAD
ABSOLUTE HERO

VALERIE TRIPP

Illustrated by Geneva Bowers

UNDER THE *Stars*

NATIONAL
GEOGRAPHIC

Since 1888, the National Geographic Society has funded more than 12,000 research, exploration, and preservation projects around the world. The Society receives funds from National Geographic Partners, LLC, funded in part by your purchase. A portion of the proceeds from this book supports this vital work. To learn more, visit natgeo.com/info.

NATIONAL GEOGRAPHIC and Yellow Border Design are trademarks of the National Geographic Society, used under license.

Under the Stars is a trademark of National Geographic Partners, LLC.

For more information, visit nationalgeographic.com, call 1-877-873-6846, or write to the following address:

National Geographic Partners
1145 17th Street N.W.
Washington, D.C. 20036-4688 U.S.A.

Visit us online at nationalgeographic.com/books

For librarians and teachers: nationalgeographic.com/books/librarians-and-educators/

More for kids from National Geographic: natgeokids.com

National Geographic Kids magazine inspires children to explore their world with fun yet educational articles on animals, science, nature, and more. Using fresh storytelling and amazing photography, *Nat Geo Kids* shows kids ages 6 to 14 the fascinating truth about the world—and why they should care. **kids.nationalgeographic.com/subscribe**

For rights or permissions inquiries, please contact National Geographic Books Subsidiary Rights: bookrights@natgeo.com

Designed by Julide Dengel
Illustrations by Geneva Bowers

Hardcover ISBN: 978-1-4263-3869-4
Reinforced library binding ISBN: 978-1-4263-3870-0

Printed in the United States of America
20/WOR/1

For Barbara Peck Rothrock,
the best BFF ever,
with all my love.
—Valerie Tripp

Dedicated to all the future
smart squads out there.
—Geneva Bowers

Izzy Newton let go.

The rope swing went slack, and for a moment, for one heartbeat, Izzy was suspended in air. *Yes!* she thought. *This is how it feels to be weightless.* Then gravity took over. Down she plummeted, slipping smoothly into the water toes first. She landed on the soft, muddy lake bottom and then thrust herself up, bursting into the fire-bright sunshine. *Air, water, earth, fire,* she thought happily. *All four elements in a row. How often can you experience that?*

"*Yah-hoo,* Izzy!" cheered her friends Charlie Darwin and Allie Einstein, who were treading water nearby. The girls had biked to the lake for the last swim of the summer. Tomorrow was the first day of school, and they wanted to soak up every possible minute of being outdoors, preferably at the lake. Actually, preferably *in* the lake.

Allie churned up waves to splash Izzy in celebration. "You did it," she shouted. *"Finally!"*

"¡Hurra!" yelled Charlie. "Way to go, Izzy!"

"Admit it: You loved it," said Allie.

"I did," Izzy agreed. She nodded, sending water droplets sliding down her nose. Other droplets that were caught in her eyelashes and her curly black hair refracted the sunlight like prisms. "You're right. The rope swing is The Best."

"I can't *believe* it took you all summer to jump!" said Allie. "You're such a chicken!"

"Hey," Charlie protested. "First of all, chickens aren't necessarily scaredy-cats. And neither is Izzy. She's just, like, you know, slow and careful. Right, Iz?"

"Yeeesss," said Izzy, slowly and carefully. In slo-mo, she cupped her hands and, with exaggerated care, scooped up water and sprinkled it on her friends.

The three girls burst into laughter.

Izzy knew she wasn't the bravest person in the world. Take the rope swing, for example. It was a brand-new addition to the lake this summer. The very first time Allie and Charlie saw it, their eyes lit up and they raced over to test it out. Not Izzy. The first time and *every* time she'd thought about trying the swing, she'd held back. Questions flashed through her brain and set it whirling: *What if I let go too soon? What if I belly flop? Would all the other swimmers watch and laugh at me?* No wonder her nickname was "Dizzy Izzy"; her mind was always spinning.

But tomorrow was a new day—her first at Atom Middle School—and Izzy was determined to leave Dizzy Izzy behind. It may have taken all summer, but Izzy felt that her leap off the rope swing was a giant step toward ditching her anxious alter ego. She grinned at her friends and said, "Now that I've jumped once, I want to do it again—like a gazillion more times."

"Me too!" said Allie, already wading ashore. Allie was too impatient to walk the long curve of the beach past the lifeguard's chair and wait her turn behind the other kids headed to the tree. She took a more direct route, scrambling over the rocks at the tree's base.

"Allie," Charlie called out in warning, "I think that might be—"

But Allie was already too far away to hear Charlie. She grabbed the rope, ran back and then forward, and swung out over the water. *"Waa-hoo!"* she whooped, wildly waving her arms and legs as she tumbled through the air into the water, making as much commotion as possible.

Charlie sighed, saying, "Gotta feel sorry for the poor fish, don't you?"

"Yup," said Izzy. She grinned. It was typical of Charlie to sympathize with the lake creatures.

"Hurry *up,*" commanded Allie when she surfaced next to Izzy and Charlie. "Today's your last chance to do those gazillion jumps, Izzy. Tomorrow is the first day of school."

"I know," said Izzy. "And not just *any* first day. Tomorrow's the first day of *middle* school."

"Claro," said Charlie. "So, Izzy, if you don't want to show up covered in a rash, don't climb over the rocks like Allie Oop just did." Charlie pointed to some greenery growing on the rocks. "That's poison ivy."

"No way!" squeaked Allie.

"Yes way," said Charlie.

"Isn't it pachysandra?" asked Allie.

Charlie shook her head. "Poison," she repeated, "ivy."

"Awww, man!" groaned Allie, frantically examining her arms. "Just what I need for the first day of school:

a screaming pink rash."

"I tried to stop you," said Charlie, "but—"

"You were too rash!" joked Izzy. "Get it?"

"Ha, ha," said Allie, rolling her eyes at Izzy's painful pun.

"Never mind, Allie," soothed Charlie. "The lake water will wash the poison ivy off. Wait here while Izzy and I jump again."

"Let's go the long way, Charlie," said Izzy. She slid Allie a grin and scratched an imaginary itch behind her ear. "A pink rash will clash with my back-to-school outfit."

"Ohhhh," moaned Allie with dramatic misery. She sank down into the water until it covered her bright blond head and then shot up right next to Izzy to splash her, laughing loudly.

Good old Allie, thought Izzy. *Talk about a disaster magnet! But she bounces back fast.* Charlie, on the other hand, was just naturally cool and calm. Izzy watched Charlie use the rope swing: Effortlessly, she swooped, flipped midair, and dove smoothly. Izzy had to give her own jump a lot more thought. She carefully calculated when the swing reached its highest point and then, just as carefully, let go and slipped into the water, trying to make as small a splash as possible.

As she waded ashore, Izzy shivered. "Am I crazy, or does the lake feel warmer than the air?"

"I mean … you *are* crazy," said Allie. "But you're also right. It's pretty cold for September. Seems like the temperature's dropping every day! The leaves will probably change color early this year."

"Well," Izzy corrected, "that also has to do with the angle of the sun and hours of sunlight." Izzy knew all about the sun, moon, stars, and planets; she loved space! Her grandfather taught physics—the study of energy and what things are made of—at the local college. Sometimes he and Izzy used the telescope there to stargaze. Izzy was saving up to buy a telescope of her own. Her ambition was to discover a star so that she could name it after Granddad. Ever since Izzy was a little girl, he had encouraged her fascination with light, heat, sound, electricity, motion, and force. Izzy was determined to be a physicist just like him when she grew up.

The girls waded up the sloping beach to the shore.

"Anyone hungry?" asked Charlie, offering snacks.

"No, thank you," said Allie and Izzy together, quickly. Charlie and her family—her two moms and her two younger brothers—had a small vegetable garden. Her snacks were always homegrown and a little *too* healthy. The kale chips she'd brought today were no exception. "You sure?" asked Charlie, her mouth full of green. When Izzy and Allie shook their heads emphatically, she shrugged. "Your loss."

"No offense, Charlie," joked Izzy, "but those kale chips look—and smell—like mulch."

Charlie laughed and shoveled another handful into her mouth. "Yum," she said with a sly wink. "Delicious."

"Speaking of delicious," said Izzy. "I told Granddad I'd help him get dinner ready. So I better head home."

"Izzy, wait till you tell your granddad you tackled the rope swing today," said Allie as she crammed her wet towel into her backpack.

"You didn't just tackle it," added Charlie. "You ACED it!"

"He'll be proud," said Allie.

"Yup, he will," said Izzy as she and her friends hopped on their bikes and started down the lane. It was true: Izzy's granddad was her biggest fan. After every A-plus report card, every "100% Perfect!" sticker on every quiz, Granddad was the first one waiting with a high five. Nobody believed in Izzy more than Granddad. Now, if she could just bring him with her to sixth-grade homeroom tomorrow. "You know, guys," Izzy admitted to Charlie and Allie riding beside her. "I'm freaked out about tomorrow."

"Me too," said Charlie.

"Me three," agreed Allie.

For a while, the girls pedaled silently. They were thinking of all the ways middle school was different from elementary school: changing classes, tons more homework, and *dances*. Tomorrow, they'd be swept up in the swirl of students flowing in from other elementary schools. There'd be lots of new faces.

"What if we aren't in the same classes?" asked Izzy. She knew she sounded Dizzy Izzy-ish, but she couldn't help worrying out loud. "How are we going to find our way around the building and get to our classes on time? What if the new kids are mean? What if we forget our homework assignments? Or locker combinations?"

"Allie," said Charlie, "you're good at numbers. Maybe you can help us remember our combinations."

"Sure," said Allie. "I'll try, anyway."

"I'm going to try out for the track team," said Charlie. "Remember, in middle school you have to try out for stuff you want to do, like teams and chorus and the school play. It's not like elementary school, where everybody does everything."

"Oh, right!" said Izzy. "My brothers said something about tryouts." Thinking about tryouts made Izzy feel wobbly on her bike. She had planned to play her favorite sport: ice hockey. She loved the physics of the blade on ice,

the speed and the momentum, and the challenge of figuring out the perfect force and timing to hit the puck into the goal. It suddenly occurred to her that she might not even *make* the team. "Thanks a lot, Charlie," she groaned. "Now I'm even *more* worried."

"Nice going, Char," said Allie. "Izzy's already crazed about tomorrow."

Tomorrow! Izzy repeated to herself. She trembled. The dreaded day was only hours away. She asked anxiously, "How will we meet up with each other in the morning before school? We should make a *plan,* a specific plan."

"Let's meet at the bike racks," said Charlie. "I'm going to ride my bike to school. Are you guys?"

Allie answered yes. But before Izzy could respond, her phone beeped. It was an old flip phone that her mom had given her for emergencies. Coasting slowly, Izzy lifted the phone out of her bike basket, flipped it open one-handed, and saw that she had a text. "Whoa," she breathed. She stopped her bike. "Intense."

"What?" asked Allie and Charlie, stopping, too.

"Guess what?" said Izzy.

"What?" asked Allie and Charlie again.

"I just got a text from my mom," said Izzy. "It's about Marie. She's back."

"Wait, *WHAT*?" gasped both Allie and Charlie.

Izzy spoke slowly and clearly. "Marie's mom texted my mom to say that they're back. They're in a new apartment, but Marie will be going to our school."

"Marie. Is. Back," stated Charlie, as if she needed to say it to believe it.

"Whoa … that *is* intense," said Allie.

"It's … it's *good* intense," said Izzy, looking at her friends. "Right?"

Charlie nodded slowly. "Sure," she said. But she sounded *un*sure.

Marie Curie had been Izzy's best friend since preschool. In elementary school, Marie and Izzy and Charlie and Allie had been a solid team. The girls had looked forward to being a fantastic fourth-grade foursome. But Marie left after third grade. She and her family had been living in Paris for the past two years.

At first, the four friends tried hard to Skype each other regularly. But it was hard. The time difference between America and France threw them off; it seemed like it was always the wrong time to talk, either way too early in the morning or way too late at night. And also, it seemed like Marie was always busy. She was traveling around Europe with her family, taking cooking classes, and exploring Paris with her cool new friends. For a while, Marie sent photos of herself in chic French clothing and weird French haircuts, made jokes in French, and referenced French celebrities, whom the other girls didn't know. Then, suddenly, Marie stopped responding to e-mails and texts. One time, the girls tried to call her and there was no answer, so they gave up. Marie was a mystery—a mystery that hurt, too.

Izzy thought aloud, "The real question is: Why didn't Marie text *us* to say she's back?"

"She dumped us," said Allie, sharp and certain. "That's why. Face it."

"Ohhh, no, I don't know," said Izzy. She hated to give up on anything, and a friendship

seemed way too important to just kick to the curb. "Don't you think we kind of fell apart because she was so far away in France? Now that she's back, maybe we'll be friends again."

"Nope," said Allie. "You can't put a positive spin on this one, Izzy. Marie stopped talking to us a long time ago. I don't know why. But it is clear that now, as far as she's concerned, we're over and out."

"I still hope—" Izzy began.

Charlie interrupted gently. "I think Marie has made it pretty clear that she isn't interested in us anymore," she said. "I think she thinks she's outgrown us. When she thinks of us, she probably remembers the goofy kid-stuff chemistry we used to do. Like, remember how we used to spend hours testing out different recipes for slime?"

"That's not kid stuff. Making slime was FUN!" protested Izzy. "It's STILL fun!"

"Fun that Marie is way too cool for now," said Charlie. "Think of the photos she sent us where she looked so French and sophisticated. She used to be all about chemistry, but not anymore, judging by those photos."

"Marie's *Marie*," said Izzy. "She'll be glad to see us."

"*Hunh!*" snorted Allie. "Don't count on it."

"Allie's right," said Charlie. "I know you don't like change, Izzy. But I think you'll only get hurt by hoping Marie will be the way she used to be. Past is past. We're not the same, and she won't be, either."

"That's one hundred percent for sure," said Allie.

"But!" said Izzy, holding up her index finger to make a point. "There *is* a fifty-fifty chance that the *new* Marie will be friendly, right?"

"I hope so," said Charlie.

"Well," said Allie, "I guess so."

"I know so," said Izzy. "Maybe she will, maybe she won't; both possibilities are equally likely. I think the friendly fifty percent possibility will win. You guys think the not-friendly fifty percent will win. We'll just have to wait and see."

Allie and Charlie exchanged a glance, eyebrows raised.

WHEN THE GIRLS REACHED IZZY'S HOUSE, CHARLIE AND ALLIE waved goodbye and Izzy went inside. She could hear her two older brothers in the kitchen goofing around as usual. So she slid into the serene silence of her own room, where there was no one to disturb her solitude but her fat old cat, Wickins, who only opened one eye to greet her, and then went back to sleep.

Izzy's room was a closet, really, with one small window and a skylight so Izzy could see the stars. Her bed was lofted up high, and her desk fit neatly in the space below. The ladder doubled as a bookshelf, her clothes fit in the desk drawers, and her ice hockey skates, backpack, and flute case hung on wall hooks. Izzy had long ago learned to take care of her possessions; anything left lying around the house was sure to be chucked between her brothers like a football and inevitably broken or lost.

As Izzy changed her clothes, she stared at a snapshot of Marie and herself that was taped to her bulletin board. Izzy thought she looked pretty much the same: wiry, with big eyes that matched her dark brown skin, a cloud of curly black hair, and a shy smile. She was shorter than Marie, who smiled at the camera with confidence. They were holding between them their third-grade science fair project, which was a balsa-wood airplane powered by rubber bands and balloons. Pinned to their shirts were the first-place ribbons they'd won. Izzy still had her ribbon. It was taped next to the photo, looking a little faded now in the narrow beam of sunlight that came in through her window.

Izzy's flute always helped her concentrate, so she took it out and began to play. The soft silvery notes usually took her mind off her troubles—but not this time.

After a while, Granddad poked his head in the door. "Your flute sounds worried," he said. "What's up?"

"Too much," said Izzy. "I don't know where to begin."

"Start where you are," said Granddad. "That's usually best." He sat at Izzy's desk and looked at her intently. He was focused and ready to listen.

"Okay, then," said Izzy. "Tomorrow is the first day of middle school, and I'm really worried."

"That seems normal to me," said Granddad.

Izzy laughed. Somehow, Granddad telling her it was okay to worry made her feel better—and oddly enough, *less* worried.

"Be specific," said Granddad. Even though she was only 11 years old and not turning 12 until January, Granddad always spoke to Izzy in a very grown-up way, scientist to scientist. Izzy loved it. "What precisely are you worried about?" asked Granddad.

"Well, for starters, I'm worried that I'll be sort of invisible because I'm so little and quiet," said Izzy.

Granddad tilted his head. "You aren't quiet *all* the time," he said. "You talk up a storm with your friends, and

I've heard you be as loud as your brothers, The Noise Boys. Listen to them in the kitchen now. They're making pizza, a mess, and a racket."

Granddad was right. Her brothers were drumming a reggae rhythm on the cooking pots and crashing lids together like cymbals.

"I mean I'm quiet with people I don't know well," said Izzy. "I'm nervous about meeting all the new people tomorrow."

"Mm-hmm," said Granddad. "With strangers you *are* quiet—on the outside, but your brain is whirring on the inside all the time. And just because you're quiet doesn't mean you have nothing to say. Quiet, introspective people have lots to contribute. You know that."

Izzy nodded.

"And I know *you*, Izzy," Granddad went on. "You feel just as passionately and you get just as excited as anybody; you just keep it inside and use it as energy, like an internal combustion engine, instead of exploding like fireworks. And you're not always shy, either. If there's something you're determined about, you speak up. Remember the decision about Wickins?"

"Oh, yeah," said Izzy, smiling. Her parents had been completely against getting a cat, but Izzy had set forth her arguments with such conviction that they had finally given in. Izzy picked Wickins up now and held him close so she could feel him purring.

"Anything else?" asked Granddad patiently.

Izzy sighed. "Marie is back from Paris. Allie, Charlie, and I haven't heard from her in a long time, but back when she *did* send us some pictures, she looked really different—super grown-up. Allie and Charlie think she's gotten so sophisticated and cool that she won't want to be our friend anymore. I don't want to believe that, but honestly I don't know what to expect."

"Now you're entering the realm of pure speculation," said Granddad. "You have no solid evidence and no firm facts. Valid conclusions can't be drawn from insufficient data."

"Well, yes," said Izzy, "but if Marie does feel the way Allie and Charlie thinks she feels, then maybe she won't want to be our friend. We won't know how to act, and—"

Granddad held up his hands. "Stop," he said. "Listen, Izzy. All scientific theory follows a rule called Occam's razor. It's a logical principle that states that you should not make more assumptions than the minimum needed. It means simplest is best. Don't assume things are more complicated than they appear. You are breaking that rule now by making lots of baseless assumptions, which only leads to needless worry." He stood up and hugged Izzy, saying, "So, meeting adjourned. Come on, Ms. Izzy. We better go to the kitchen and restore order before your brothers wreak more havoc. *That* we know is not a baseless assumption. It is a real possibility based on *lots* of past evidence and experience, right?"

"Right!" said Izzy. She put Wickins down, packed her flute away, and went off to help Granddad and the boys make dinner. As she did, she thought, *I'll have to remember that Occam's razor thing: Don't make assumptions. Don't make things more complicated than they need to be. Maybe Marie is still the same old Marie. Maybe middle school will be okay!*

The next morning, Wednesday, Izzy was so anxious about being late that she arrived at school much too early to expect to see Allie and Charlie. She pedaled her bike around the school grounds awhile to kill time. Atom Middle School was a scruffy two-story brick building that was long overdue for a renovation. Even from the outside,

Izzy wondered how 900 sixth, seventh, and eighth graders could possibly fit inside. Plans had been drawn up to expand and modernize the school with up-to-date science labs, a library with all new computers, and state-of-the-art gyms. But funds hadn't yet been allocated for the multimillion-dollar overhaul. Still, the more Izzy looked at it, the more she liked the old building. It was on a hill that sloped down to the playing fields. There were shops across the street and woods behind the building. From the parking lot, Izzy had a view of the lake. She really, *really* wished that she could rewind and have it be yesterday again, when she and Allie and Charlie were at the lake together. Her stomach was queasy, and even though it was a brisk, cool morning, her hands were sweaty on the bike handlebars.

Just then she heard someone call out, "Izzy! Yoo-hoo!" Allie skidded up and stopped next to Izzy with a screech of brakes. "Hi!" she said.

"Hi," said Izzy. "How come you're here so early?"

" 'Cause I knew that you'd be here *way* too early, so I came to keep you company," said Allie.

"Thanks." Izzy grinned.

"Plus, I'm excited," said Allie. "I mean, *middle school*, right?" She took off her bike helmet and her gorgeous white-blond hair looked as wired as she sounded. It stuck up and out all over her head in exclamation points, catching the sunlight, looking bright, electric, and exuberant. "You look great, Izzy," Allie said, and before Izzy could respond, Allie looked down and sighed, "I'm a walking disaster."

"What do you mean?" asked Izzy.

"Well, look!" Allie made a sweeping motion with her hands from her shirt downward.

She was wearing a bluish tie-dye shirt, blue jeggings, and mismatched blue socks that peeked out over her blue tennis shoes. "Bubbie decided that I'm old enough to do my own laundry," Allie explained. "So I put my new blue jeggings in the wash with lots of my socks and

T-shirts. The jeggings bled all over them and tinted them different shades of blue!"

"Blue's nice!" said Izzy.

Allie sighed again. "Oh, well," she said. "At least now all my clothes go together, so I have the greatest possible number of combinations of outfits."

"It'll make getting dressed in the morning quicker," added Izzy. "You won't have to waste time deciding what color shirt to wear. They're all—"

"Blue!" Allie chimed in cheerfully. She looked around. "It seems like there are hundreds of kids arriving, more every minute. But I don't see Char. *I'm* the one who's usually late! Oh, well. She probably got distracted by an earthworm or something."

It was true that when Charlie was watching an animal or studying an unusual plant she became so absorbed that she forgot about everything else.

"No, I bet she's here and we just can't find her," Izzy said, trying not to sound anxious. "There are lots of bike racks. We should have checked it out ahead of time and said *specifically* which one we'd meet at."

"I'll call her," said Allie, getting out her cell phone.

"Don't let a teacher see that," warned a passing student, "or it'll end up in phone jail."

"Phone jail?" repeated Allie. "What's phone jail?"

"A box in the principal's office," said the boy. "You can't get your phone back till the end of the day."

Allie quickly jammed her phone into her pocket. "*Now* what'll we do?" she asked Izzy. "How will we find Charlie? What if the bell rings and it's time to go inside? We can't be late on our first day!"

Izzy was already on edge, and Allie's questions came close to nudging her into a panic. Luckily, just then they saw Charlie rolling toward them on her bike, eating a banana that she held in her free hand. Charlie was wearing cotton pants and a T-shirt that said "Lettuce turnip the beet." She looked unruffled and unhurried, even as Allie was waving to her and shouting, "Hurry *up*!"

"I love your shirt," said Izzy. "Very vegetarian."

"Thanks," said Charlie as they all parked their bikes in the bike rack. "I wore short sleeves because last year on the first day of school I *roasted*. But I'm starting to regret it … it's chilly out today!"

When the girls entered the building, Allie shivered

and said, "Yikes! It's *freezing* in here!"

"My shirt should say 'Lettuce turnip the HEAT'!" said Charlie, rubbing her arms to warm them.

"The temperature must be absolute zero," said Izzy. Granddad had taught her that absolute zero is the coldest possible temperature. "I've got goose bumps," she continued. "But maybe that's just because I'm excited."

"Body temperature rises with emotion," said Charlie. "It doesn't sink."

Then I should be boiling, thought Izzy, *because I'm a hot mess.*

It was just as hard to walk in the busy, bustling, bulging building as Izzy had feared it would be. The halls were so jammed that the girls were shoved and buffeted, jostled and pushed, and they had to wiggle their way along the wall to get by. There were two staircases, and both of them were challenging to navigate because some students were cascading *down* while others were battling to go *up*.

"I feel like a salmon swimming my way up a waterfall," said Charlie as she and Izzy and Allie struggled up one of the staircases. Charlie was the tallest of the three girls, so she led the way. But even so, because of the congested halls and staircase, the girls were last to the auditorium for sixth-grade assembly, which was nerve-racking. And worse than *that,* they were scolded when they finally got there. "Girls, you are going to have to move faster," a teacher said, shaking her head as they skittered into the auditorium.

Allie began to protest, "We—"

"Go!" said the teacher. She waved them forward into the auditorium, saying, "Find seats."

In among the scary sea of strangers, Izzy was glad to see some faces that were familiar from her old elementary school, the lake, and even her neighborhood.

But of course, she admitted to herself, she was really searching for one face in particular: Marie's.

It was Allie who first spotted her. "Don't look now," Allie muttered. She tilted her head toward the front of the auditorium. "There's Mademoiselle Marie."

Izzy's heart lifted at the sight of her old friend. When Marie had cut off communication with her, Izzy had tried not to care so that she didn't hurt so much. Now all of her feelings for Marie came rushing back. She was so glad to see her! Marie was down by the stage. She was standing up, looking around.

"Marie is looking for us," said Izzy happily.

"Not likely," said Allie. "See that *one* empty seat next to her? She's saving it for someone. That's a no-brainer."

"Maybe," said Izzy. "But let's go say hi anyway."

"Okay." Allie shrugged. "It's your funeral."

Izzy led the way. Charlie was close behind, walking slowly as if toward an animal she didn't want to startle, and Allie was lagging last. Izzy kept her eyes on Marie's face as they went toward her. When Marie saw them, Izzy gave her a little wave. Marie didn't exactly frown, but she didn't smile, either. Her expression was a hard-to-read chemical concoction of surprise, dread, and discomfort.

"Welcome back, Marie," said Izzy. She spoke softly and reached out for a hug.

Marie stepped back, out of hugging range. "Thanks," she said flatly.

She only nodded when Charlie said, "We're happy to see you."

Allie and Marie said at the same time, "Hi."

"So! No more glasses," said Izzy, a little too heartily. "You've got contact lenses now. *Very* cool. And you don't have braces anymore, either."

"I'm still a metal mouth," said Allie, pointing to her braces. "And a motormouth, too."

Allie laughed loudly at her own joke and Izzy cringed, thinking, *Turn your volume down, Allie.* Quickly, Izzy said to Marie, "I love your new hairdo. It's The Best!"

Marie always had been very particular about her appearance, and straight-up fearless about fashion and hairdos. Today her hair had a hot pink streak from her part to her chin that matched her shirt's hot pink sequin stripes and the pink sparkles scattered across her tulle skirt. "You should be, like, a social media influencer or something!" said Izzy.

"Oh," said Marie, tucking a pink streak of hair behind one ear. "Thanks."

"And wow!" said Charlie, pointing to Marie's sneakers, which were shiny and changed colors when she moved. "How'd you make your shoes glow like that?"

"Oh," said Marie again, "phosphorescent paint."

Izzy saw that Marie was distracted, and she saw why: Two girls were staring at Izzy, Marie, Allie, and Charlie and whispering to each other. A wave of self-consciousness swept over Izzy from head to toe. Politely she said, "Listen, Marie. We're late to this assembly already because of the crowded halls. Aren't those stairs just the worst? And can you believe how cold it is in here? Anyway, we have to hustle to find seats, so we can't talk now, but can you come over after school? Granddad would love to see you! We'll make sundaes, like we used to! Or peanut butter toast or sandwiches with—what did you always call it when we were little? *Swish* cheese!"

"Thank you, Izzy," said Marie, also polite. "But no, I have to go straight home."

"We could come to your house," suggested Charlie.

"No," Marie said again. "That won't work."

"Oh, right," said Charlie. "I remember that your mom always was sort of strict." Marie's mom kept the house "just so" at all times and decorated it elaborately.

Izzy piped up, "Remember that time we made an explosion in your kitchen and blew the fuses and all your Christmas lights went out? Your mom was pretty mad about it. So I guess—"

"Look," Marie said abruptly, "I'll talk to you guys later."

"Oh! Okay," said Izzy, Charlie, and Allie together, all three taken aback by Marie's coldness.

Sometimes, when Izzy was anxious, she made dumb jokes. This was one of those times. She grinned too wide and said goodbye to Marie the way they used to when they were in third grade: "See you later, alligator!"

Charlie understood that Izzy was nervously trying to

remind Marie of the fun they used to have. She laughed kindly and said, "*¡Vale!* Okay, Izzy! We're not in third grade anymore, but I'll pick up my cue. I say, 'In a while, crocodile.' Right?"

Not one to miss a beat, Allie chimed in, "And I say, 'See you soon, raccoon!'"

They waited for Marie to say, "In an hour, sunflower!"

When she didn't, Allie said, in an exaggeratedly bad French accent, "*Au revoir,* minotaur! That's a French one I made up for you, Marie."

Marie winced, and Izzy saw that the two staring girls were snickering at them now. "Yes, well," Marie said curtly, "as Charlie said, we're not in third grade anymore. I'll see you around." She turned away and sat down.

"Yikes," said Allie as she and Charlie and Izzy walked back up the aisle. "I'd say I told you so, but that was even *more* awkward than I thought it would be."

Even Izzy had to admit, "Marie didn't exactly seem overjoyed to see us."

"Ya think?" said Allie. "*That's* the understatement of the century."

"It's like she's Marie's evil twin," said Charlie. She

sighed. "Well, there's no way we can stop her from being different from the way she used to be. She has evolved."

Izzy felt torn in two. Part of her still believed that Marie wanted to be their friend, even if she had changed in other ways. But after that encounter, part of her couldn't shake off this nagging, negative thought: *One law of physics is that every action has an equal and opposite reaction. Marie certainly had an equal and opposite reaction to our warm friendliness: a very cold shoulder.*

Izzy glanced back and saw Marie wave to someone— a new girl that Izzy didn't recognize—and motion the girl toward her and the seat that she had saved. The new girl had snappy brown eyes. She wore eyeglasses with big frames and overalls with lots of pockets. Marie spoke animatedly and intently to her as they took their seats next to one another. It was clear to see Marie had no cold shoulder for the new girl.

For a second, Izzy was crushed. Then her determined streak kicked in, and she thought, *I don't know how, but Allie, Charlie, and I will warm Marie up. We'll make her want to be our friend again.*

Izzy, Allie, and Charlie found three seats together in the back of the auditorium and plunked themselves down just as the principal, Mr. Delmonico, began to speak to the 300 new sixth graders. He was a beanpole, but his voice was big and booming as he said, "All right, let's settle down now." The noise didn't decrease at all, so Mr. Delmonico tried again. "Students! Atom Middle School sixth graders! Your attention, please!" When that didn't work, the principal resorted to flicking the lights on and off and bellowing, "Quiet!"

Finally, with lots of rustling, whispers, and squeaking seats, the room quieted.

"Thank you," said the principal. "I'm Mr. Delmonico. I'm new here at Atom Middle School, too, so you and I will begin together. Let's get off to a good start."

"Why's it so cold?" someone yelled, and everyone cheered and whistled in support of the question. "It's cold outside, but it's *freeeeezing* in here!"

Mr. Delmonico shook his head. "I know," he said. He shivered. "I'm cold, too. Maintenance is working on it. This is an old building, and we've had some trouble with the air-conditioning unit. It's like the thing's got a mind of its own. But never fear, technicians are in my office today checking out the thermostat. We should be back to normal in no time."

At that, someone started a wave that swept across the auditorium, with kids standing up, waving their hands in the air, and saying, "Brrrr!" This was met with gales of laughter.

"Let's keep it down to a dull roar, folks!" said Mr. Delmonico, though he had a chuckle in his voice. When the laughter died down, he continued, saying, "The purpose of this morning's assembly is to welcome you to Atom Middle School and to go over the school rules and expectations. There's really only one rule: Be kind. And I have only one expectation: Follow the rule. Now, you've been assigned to homerooms alphabetically by last name. Your homeroom teachers will hand out your schedules, locker assignments, and combinations."

Nervous murmurs rippled through the auditorium.

Mr. Delmonico spoke over the anxious muttering. "I know that lockers and locker combinations are new for most of you. But you'll get used to them. Stay cool."

"Cool?" shouted out a girl. "We're frozen."

"What's our school mascot?" called out a kid. "Polar bears? Arctic wolves?"

Someone howled like a wolf, and everyone laughed.

Izzy felt sorry for Mr. Delmonico. He seemed like a nice guy. He was new at Atom Middle School, just like all the sixth graders were. And it wasn't *his* fault the school was too cold for comfort.

Mr. Delmonico waited for the laugher to subside. Then he said patiently, "No. Our teams are the Atomics. Speaking of, teams and clubs will have sign-up sheets at tables in the cafeteria tomorrow at lunchtime. Check with team captains and club leaders for tryout schedules."

"*Tryouts!*" Izzy whispered to Charlie, making a worried face. "So *soon.*"

Charlie nodded, but kept silent.

Mr. Delmonico went on. "If you want to start a club, bring a sign-up sheet to the cafeteria tomorrow. Okay, it's time to head to your homerooms. Teachers, hold up your posters. Students, go stand by the teacher whose poster has the first letter of your last name on it."

The auditorium erupted in chaos as 300 students jumped up from their seats and stampeded toward the teachers. Mr. Delmonico shouted, "Walk, please!" But no one did. Allie and Charlie waved to Izzy as they headed off in one direction toward the teacher holding the D-E-F poster and Izzy headed in the other direction toward the teacher with the N-O-P poster. Allie pointed to herself and Charlie, and then to Izzy, and mimed eating, which Izzy interpreted to mean: *See you at lunch.* Izzy nodded vigorously to show her agreement. Out of the corner of her eye, she saw both Marie and the new girl heading toward the teacher with the A-B-C poster. Their heads were bent close together, and they were laughing and talking to one another as if, thought Izzy with a small silent sigh, they were the only two girls in the world.

Izzy felt dizzy.

When her homeroom teacher handed out their schedules, Izzy saw that classes were on a block schedule. That meant that some classes met Monday, Wednesday, and Friday and others met Tuesday and Thursday—unless it was a half day, in which case all bets were off and for some reason the Monday schedule went into effect but classes met for only 20 minutes each. Also, students were assigned to something called electives, which was weird because no one elected what elective to take. The electives had names like "Humanities," "Creative Expression," and "Art History." Izzy was happy to see that she had been assigned to an elective called "Forensics" that met Tuesdays and Thursdays. Forensics sounded right up her alley: She loved the idea of using the scientific method to solve crimes. She knew that's what Forensics meant because she'd seen lots of TV shows about it.

When homeroom was over, Izzy braced herself, hunched her shoulders, and burrowed her way through the crowded hallway, afraid she'd be late for her first class, which was Math. But when she arrived at the classroom, she saw that the teacher wasn't there yet. Izzy was glad to see Allie in the classroom. There was no seat open near

Allie, and as Izzy hesitated by the door, a gangly boy smiled at her and pointed to the empty seat in front of him.

"Here's a seat," he said.

"Thanks," said Izzy.

As she sat, the boy said, "I'm Trevor. I just moved here, and—"

But just then, Allie shouted, "Izzy! Watch this!"

Allie stood up in front of her desk. "It's COLD in here!" she said. Her big eyes sparkled and her zingy hair bounced. Allie flung one arm wide and pretended that her thermos was a microphone that she held in front of

her mouth. At top volume, she began singing the song from the movie *Frozen* except she changed the words to *"Let it snow, let it snow ..."* And then Allie tossed a handful of white paper torn into confetti over her head so that it snowed down on her.

Oh, Allie! Izzy squirmed with embarrassment. This wasn't the first time Izzy wished that Allie wasn't an aspiring stand-up comedian. Izzy was relieved when everyone clapped, stamped, and cheered. A boy had started to sing the old song "Walking in a Winter Wonderland" when the teacher, Ms. Tattinger, walked in.

Luckily, Ms. Tattinger had a sense of humor. "It *is* awfully cold outside and also in this building," she said. "But not quite cold enough to snow, outside or inside. Anyway, we're here to do math. Pick up the confetti paper, and let's begin."

As Ms. Tattinger wrote math problems on the board, Izzy felt a wonderful sense of calm come over her. Math was neat and tidy. It made sense. It wasn't about messy stuff like hurt feelings and old friendships. Izzy might not solve the math problems as fast as Allie did, and she was way, *way* too shy to shout out the answers like Allie did, but she was sure of what she was doing, and she loved the quiet satisfaction of finding the correct solution. When Ms. Tattinger called on Izzy to solve an especially tricky problem and Izzy was able to find the right answer, Trevor leaned forward and whispered, "Nice."

Izzy looked down shyly, but she grinned happily, too!

On the way to lunch, the halls were even *more* crowded than before because mechanics had set up ladders at various places in the corridors. They were inspecting the overhead ducts, the wall vents, and the pipes that ran under the floors. Students whistled "Jingle Bells" and chanted "Snow day! Snow day!" as they slalomed their way around the construction.

"The whole cafeteria is as cold as a refrigerator," joked Izzy as she, Charlie, and Allie sat down at a table together. "I don't know why they bother keeping the milk in a cooler. They should just keep a cow outside in the parking lot, or in here. I mean, look around. Everyone's so frostbitten that they look like they're on a field trip to an ice floe in Antarctica."

"I don't know why they can't figure out what's wrong with the heating in this place," said Allie, waving her sandwich around so that the tomatoes slipped out. "Why is it such a mystery?"

"That's not the only mystery," said Charlie, who was unpacking her lunch from a grocery bag. She rolled her eyes right, to draw Izzy's and Allie's attention to where Marie and the new girl sat huddled together at a table far away.

"*Humpf,*" scoffed Allie, her mouth full of sandwich. "Didn't I tell you guys this yesterday? To Marie, we're nothing. She made that crystal clear at the assembly this morning! Mystery, *shmyshtery.*"

"Hey!" said Izzy, "speaking of mysteries, guess what? I really lucked out with my English elective. I got Forensics. I'm going to be just like all those crime-solving detectives on TV!"

"Uh-oh," said Allie. Now her face looked tragic.

"Uh-oh what?" asked Izzy.

"Oh, Izzy," said Charlie sadly, "I hate to be the one to tell you this. But, well, in the case of the English elective, 'forensics' means making speeches and debating."

"Not collecting hairs and fingernails and doing DNA tests," added Allie.

"*What?*" gasped Izzy. There was nothing in the world she was more afraid of than standing up in front of people and making a speech! "How can I get out of that class?"

"I don't think you can," said Charlie. "It would throw off your whole schedule."

"They call it an 'elective,' but I NEVER would have elected it!" wailed Izzy.

"Maybe you could talk to your guidance counselor," said Allie, "and ask to be transferred. But you're going to have to take Forensics at some point this year. So you might as well get it over with."

"But," Izzy sputtered, "I'm—"

Izzy didn't have a chance to finish her sentence because three kids came over to ask Allie for help. Word was already out that Allie could remember your locker combination and figure out ways to help *you* remember it, too.

At the same time, a bunch of runners came over to make sure that Charlie was going to try out for the track and field team. Evidently, Charlie's reputation for speed had followed her to middle school. As the boys in the group talked to Charlie, Izzy saw without surprise that they stumbled over their words and got kind of red in the face. Izzy had seen this happen many times before. Charlie was so beautiful—with her wide hazel eyes—that boys lost their train of thought and forgot what they were saying when they looked at her. Charlie herself was completely oblivious to the effect she had on people and stayed unruffled, no matter what. Right now, she listened to the boys, but Izzy could tell she was really paying more attention to her lunch, which resembled a small vegetable garden that had been planted in a bento box.

No one came to talk to Izzy. But that was a good thing: She was so bummed out—and terrified—about Forensics that she wouldn't have been able to talk anyway! She looked over at Marie and the new girl talking happily to one another. Izzy was filled with a sense of longing. In the old days, Marie would have known just what to say to calm Izzy and figure out what to do about the dreaded Forensics.

But not now.

Granddad had told Izzy about a phenomenon in physics called a black hole. He explained that if you shrink a large mass—*like my friendship with Marie,* thought Izzy—enough, it becomes a black hole that has so much mass that not even light can escape its warp. The center of a black hole was called a singularity. Izzy thought that "singularity" was the loneliest word she'd ever heard. And right now, even though she was sitting at a lunch table with her friends and was surrounded by noisy kids, somehow Izzy felt exactly like a singularity.

The weather was still unseasonably cold the next day.
But as Izzy, Allie, and Charlie walked into school, it felt
colder inside the building than out! A boy behind them
said in a deep announcer's voice, "Welcome to Day Two of
the Atom Middle School freeze-out crisis." It was Trevor.

Without thinking, Izzy came back with "Everyone's
wondering: How low can it go, temperature-wise?" At the
same instant, she and Trevor both said, "Absolute zero!"

"Good one!" Allie howled. "You two should put on a
comedy show or something! Go on the road! Together!"

Eeek, shrieked Izzy inside her head. She went hot
with embarrassment.

But Trevor just grinned and waved and walked away
saying, "See you later."

With her elbow, Allie nudged Izzy so hard that Izzy was thrown off balance. "*That* boy is cute," she said. "And he's interested in y-o-u, Isabelle Newton, my friend."

Izzy blushed. "No, no—he's nice to everyone," she said.

"Mm-hmm, sure," said Allie, "but mostly he's nice to *you*."

"Too far, too fast, Al," said Charlie. "You're making Izzy uncomfortable, can't you see?"

"Sorrr-eee," said Allie, miffed.

"Come on, Miss Matchmaker," Izzy teased. She linked her arm through Allie's. "We'd better get a move on or we'll be late."

"This whole middle-school thing about switching classes and getting to class on time is hard," said Charlie. She and Izzy and Allie were so squeezed together in the center of the crowd of students clogging the hallway that they could hardly breathe. "I feel like we're some sort of six-legged, six-armed, three-headed monster creature."

Allie nodded. "Three and a half minutes is *not* enough time to get from one classroom to another," she said.

"*Not* for this volume of bodies in motion," added Izzy.

"*Especially* on the stairs," added Charlie. One kid was trying to slide down the banister so as to avoid the herd on the stairs. The stairs were another middle-school thing. Unlike their all-on-one-floor elementary school, Atom Middle School had three levels: basement, first floor, and second floor. Today the traffic jam on both staircases was significantly worse than the day before because kids had wised up about how cold it was in the building. They were wearing puffy winter coats, and so they took up even *more* space. Students weren't supposed to wear coats and jackets in class, but it was so cold in the school that teachers had made an exception.

"After someone solves the mystery of why the school is cold, someone should solve the problem of the stairs," said Charlie.

"I wish *somebody* would," agreed Allie, "and soon, before we're all squashed flat."

"Well," Izzy admitted, "today's the first day of Forensics, so I'd love to be squashed flat; that sounds like more fun than making speeches."

"Oh, Izzy!" Allie exclaimed. "I'm sorry. I forgot. You must be nervous."

"You'll do just fine," Charlie reassured her. "I'm sure."

"Me too," said Izzy with a twisted grin. "Not."

The girls parted, and then Charlie called out to Izzy, "Want a snack to calm your nerves?"

"No, thanks!" Izzy called back. She was so jittery that the *last* thing she could do was scarf down some kale chips; she'd choke! Izzy slunk into the Forensics classroom and took a seat in the back. *I told Granddad I was worried I might be invisible,* she thought. *Now I wish I were.*

It turned out that Forensics was not as bad as Izzy had expected it to be. It was worse. First, she had to stand up and say her name and tell what elementary school she was from, which made her totally nervous. She knew she sounded very Dizzy Izzy-ish as she stumbled along, mumbling, "I'm Izzy, I mean Isabelle Longview, I mean Newton from Elementary School, I mean Longview."

Everyone snickered.

Ms. Martinez, the teacher, just said, "Okay! Next?" But Izzy saw her make a note in her attendance book.

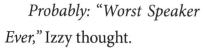

Probably: "Worst Speaker Ever," Izzy thought.

"The first rule of Forensics is: Have something you want to say," said Ms. Martinez. "You can't speak with conviction unless you care about your topic. So today, I want you to make a list of topics you'll research and then prepare and deliver a speech about."

Izzy felt as though she had swallowed a stone. *Oh, help!* she thought miserably. She opened her notebook, took out a piece of paper, and stared at the blank page. All around her other students were scribbling madly, churning out ideas.

Ms. Martinez walked up and down the aisles looking at the students' papers and chatting briefly with them about what they had written. When she came to Izzy and saw that Izzy had written nothing, Ms. Martinez tapped Izzy's paper. "Come on, Izzy," she said. "Your paper is empty, but I'm sure that your brain isn't. I'm not asking for a long list. Just one idea that you feel strongly about and have something to say about will do."

"Okay," Izzy croaked. Ms. Martinez moved on. *One idea?* thought Izzy. *Sure, I do* have one idea I feel strongly *about and have something to say—in fact, shout—about. It's the same idea I had before: Isn't there* ANY *way I can get out of this class?*

If Izzy was hoping for a calm time after Forensics, lunchtime was not it. The scene in the cafeteria was wild. Seventh and eighth graders recruiting for teams and clubs had taken over. They had taped labels to tables with the names of their clubs and teams. They stood on chairs shouting out encouragement to the sixth graders, saying, "Line up to sign up!" Members of the French Club wore paper berets and handed out French fries. Rock climbers demoed their gear, yoga clubbers twisted themselves into pretzels, and the volleyball team was tossing mini volleyballs to one another across the cafeteria. A few members of the Marching Band had set up in the corner and were playing and dancing to the Atom Middle School's fight song, which was, of course, "The Electric Slide."

Several teachers and Mr. Delmonico roamed the room keeping an eye on everybody. In the throng, Izzy spotted Charlie eating an energy bar and doing warm-up stretches with the track team at their table. Allie bounced from the Homecoming Committee table to the tables for Math Club, Pep Squad, Orchestra, Jazz Dance, and Chorus—far too many activities to handle. *Although if any human being could do it, that person would be Allie,* thought Izzy, watching her energetic friend.

After Izzy signed up to play her flute in the Marching Band, she went from table to table, too. She looked for Marie's name on every sign-up sheet but never saw it. She looked for a table for the ice hockey team, too, and didn't see that, either, so she went to the table for the girls' field hockey team and patiently waited in line. Izzy was interested to see Marie and her new friend standing near the line, clearly arguing about whether to sign up or not.

When it was Izzy's turn, the seventh grader at the table handed her a clipboard. "Print your name," said the seventh grade girl to Izzy.

"Oh," said Izzy shyly. "I … I'm not … I just wanted to ask: Where do I sign up to try out for the ice hockey team?"

All the girls at and near the table, including Marie and her friend, stared at Izzy.

"First of all," said the seventh grader, sounding superior,

"ice hockey is a winter sport, so those tryouts won't be until later. Second, girls don't play ice hockey."

"Oh," said Izzy again. She burned with self-consciousness. And something else made her hot, too: her stubborn streak. "Well," she said, "I do."

"Not in middle school you won't," dismissed the girl. She looked behind Izzy and said, "Who's next?"

Izzy pivoted and left. Gratefully, she joined Charlie and Allie, who were sitting on the floor in a corner, eating their lunches.

"How can you possibly be *sweaty*?" Charlie asked as Izzy swiped at her forehead with her palm. "It's freezing in here! My yogurt's turned into frozen yogurt."

Izzy explained what the seventh-grade girl at the field hockey table had said.

Allie made a face at the girl, which luckily the girl did not see. "Seventh-grade snob," Allie said.

"You weren't even asking to sign up for field hockey," said Charlie.

"I signed up for *every*thing," said Allie merrily. "I figure, go for broke!"

"You know what's strange?" said Izzy. "I looked at all

the sign-up sheets, and Marie's not on any of them."

"I know," said Allie. "I checked them, too, and I noticed the same thing. Why not, do you think?"

"It's beyond me," said Izzy.

"I can't believe she's not interested in *anything* offered here," added Charlie, waving her spoon in an arc at the room. "That's weird."

Mr. Delmonico clapped his hands for attention and called out, "Last call. Time's just about up. Remember, team tryouts are tomorrow, Friday afternoon, after school. If you signed up, show up. Before we end, any suggestions for new clubs?"

"Yeah!" called out a seventh grader. "How about a Heat Wave Club to warm up this meat locker of a building?"

"How about a club called The Ice Breakers?" shouted out another kid.

"I think we need a Cryobiology Club to figure out how we can survive in here," added another.

Mr. Delmonico nodded wearily. Izzy felt a wave of sympathy for him. She could tell that he was really tired of jokes about being cold. "We're working on the cold problem," he said. "Any *serious* suggestions for new clubs?"

Izzy had an inspiration. "Hey," she whispered to Allie and Charlie, "Marie always loved chemistry and science-y stuff as much as we do. What if we had a STEM team? Do you think Marie would join that?"

"I don't know about snooty Marie," said Allie, "but I'd join it in a flash. Suggest it." She ripped a blank page out of her notebook and shoved it and a pen toward Izzy. "Use this as your sign-up sheet."

"Oh no!" whispered Izzy, leaning back, both palms raised. "I couldn't!" She hated to call attention to herself. Talking at the field hockey table had been agonizing enough. She couldn't possibly stand up in front of the whole cafeteria and talk all by herself. She absolutely, positively could not. "*You* suggest it," she said to Allie.

"No way, no how," said Allie. "I'm not taking credit for your good idea."

"Me either," said Charlie. "Don't overthink this, Izzy. Pretend you're jumping off the rope swing and just *do* it. *Buena suerte.*"

Izzy's stomach tied itself in knots. She shook her head no. But then she thought: *What if a STEM team was a way—what if it was the ONLY way—to reach out to Marie?*

With all her heart, Izzy wanted to reconnect to Marie. She remembered what Granddad had said: *If there's something you're determined about, you speak up.*

So Izzy took the pen and paper from Allie. Then she took a deep breath, gathered her courage, and stood up. Behind her on either side, Allie and Charlie nudged each other and opened their eyes wide in happy astonishment. But it was so noisy and chaotic in the lunchroom that no one noticed Izzy. So Charlie put her fingers in her mouth and blew an ear-piercing whistle, and Allie jumped up and down yelling, "Hey, hey, HEY!" Out of the corner of her eye, Izzy saw Trevor flicking the lights on and off.

When the kids got quiet, Allie shouted, "Take it, Izzy!"

Izzy thought she might throw up.

"Yes?" said Mr. Delmonico, looking at Izzy.

He wasn't the only one. In fact, it seemed to Izzy that every head in the room turned toward her. This was her nightmare. Knees shaking and voice squeaky, Izzy said, "How about ... how about a STEM team?"

"That's a good idea," said Mr. Delmonico. "Funds are tight. Budget may be a problem, so I'll have to ask the school board to approve. I'll tell you what; why don't you do some research about STEM teams for me that I can share with the board. Anybody else interested in a STEM team? Give me a quick show of hands."

Allie waved both arms, whooping, *"Woo-oooo!"* Charlie raised her hand; it happened to have a bunch of grapes dangling from it. Trevor raised his hand, and then some other kids did, too. Izzy held her breath and, *Yes!* she thought joyfully, because Marie raised her hand as well.

Mr. Delmonico said, "Okay, everybody's who's interested in a STEM team, go see ..." He turned back to Izzy, asking, "What's your name?"

"Izzy Newton," said Izzy. Her voice was faint, but it didn't matter because Allie and Charlie called it out with her at the same time.

"Go see Izzy Newton and write your name on her sign-up sheet," said Mr. Delmonico. As kids headed over to do so, he went on, "I'm not saying it's a definite go, but the more names on the list, the more the board is likely to approve it. Include the list with your research, Izzy."

Izzy nodded. Allie flung her arm around Izzy's shoulder with a smile a mile wide, and Charlie tilted her head toward where Marie was standing. Izzy looked at Marie and met her glance. Was that an infinitesimal smile on Marie's face? Yup. But it didn't last long; the new girl next to Marie said something to her and Marie's smile slipped off fast.

But, *Oh, boy!* thought Izzy, pleased to have caught Marie's interest. Izzy sat at the end of a cafeteria table. She printed **STEM TEAM** at the top of the paper and under it she wrote: 1. Izzy Newton. Then she turned the paper around and handed the pen to the first kid crowded up next to the table. Allie took charge of the rest of the kids who wanted to sign up, corralling them into one orderly line. Charlie sat next to Izzy and instructed everyone to print neatly so that all the names would be legible.

Izzy was hardly aware of the happy commotion. She felt weak with relief and, at the same time, proud. It might seem insignificant to other people, but to Izzy, her victory over shyness was huge. *It was,* she thought happily, *one small victory for friendship.*

Right after lunch, Izzy went to her locker to put the sign-up sheet away. It had 24 names on it. Marie had not signed the sheet, but Izzy was sure she'd show up if the STEM team took off. Izzy's locker was easy to find because it was near the cafeteria, in the same hall as Allie's and Charlie's lockers. And her combination was easy to remember: 3-14-16, which was *pi,* rounded to the nearest ten-thousandth. Then Izzy went to the Girls' Room, which was even more of a freezer than the cafeteria. Izzy was surprised the water in the toilets hadn't turned to ice! She was in a stall when she heard two girls come in.

"So that's the girl you told me about, right?" Izzy heard an unfamiliar voice say. "That intense girl?"

"Mm-hmm," the other girl answered.

"She's out there! I mean, it's like she just didn't get the memo about what's cool and uncool in middle school," the new voice went on. "She wants to be on the ice hockey team? And on top of that, she's a science nerd. I'm like, 'Whoa! That girl's *toxic*.' Hey, by the way, I saw you raise your hand, but you know you can't join that STEM team thing of hers, right? It's impossible."

The other girl's response was lost in the rush of water as the girls washed their hands. But it didn't matter. Izzy knew that the girls had been talking about *her.* She froze solid in the stall, because when she looked down, she saw *Marie's glowing shoes!* And then she heard Marie say, "Come over to my house this afternoon. We'll hang out."

"Okay," said the new girl as she and Marie left the Girls' Room together.

Izzy leaned her forehead against the cold metal door of the stall, thinking: *So the new girl can go to Marie's house and have fun, but Charlie, Allie, and I can't. And what's worse, Allie's right: Marie thinks I'm a giant loser.*

So, should she give up her hopes for renewing her old friendship with Marie? Izzy didn't know. But Izzy was sure that there couldn't be any worse feeling in the world than thinking that she'd lost an old friend, especially one who used to really *get* her and like her in all her weirdness—a friend who liked the *real* Izzy and seemed to know that real Izzy better than she did herself. It was unusual to have a friend who liked you *because* of your unique quirkiness, down to your soul. That's who Marie had been. That's whom Izzy was pretty sure she'd lost. Because Marie now thought Izzy was a dork, somebody to avoid because she was—what was the word the new girl had used? *Toxic.*

The next day, Friday, was blissfully Forensics free.
Izzy, Allie, and Charlie all stayed after school. Charlie bundled up in a hoodie and vest because of the cold weather outside and headed to the field to try out for the track team. Allie set out on a marathon of club meetings. Izzy went to the library and media center to gather information about STEM teams to present to Mr. Delmonico.

Izzy always loved libraries. They were usually quiet but humming with ideas and, best of all, full of Izzy's favorite stuff: books, computers, and other things to read. Since it was after school, there were lots of kids in the library playing games on the computers and doing homework even though it was uncomfortably cold;

there seemed to be a polar vortex whistling through the bookstacks. Izzy saw Trevor sitting on the floor near the windows, but he had the hood of his parka pulled up and was so deep into his book that she didn't think he saw her. Izzy noticed that Trevor was reading *Harry Potter and the Prisoner of Azkaban,* which was her favorite book in the series. She reminded herself not to tell Allie that she and Trevor liked the same book. Allie was sure to read too much into *that* fact.

"May I help you?" asked Ms. Okeke, the Atom Middle School librarian and media specialist. She was tall, and her bright blue *gele* made her even taller.

"Yes, please," answered Izzy. "I'm looking for information about STEM teams."

Ms. Okeke smiled. "You are the girl who suggested a team, aren't you?"

Izzy nodded.

"The school I worked in back in Nigeria sent a team to the global competition," said Ms. Okeke. "Come on. Let's find information to convince Mr. Delmonico and the school board that Atom Middle School should have a team, too."

With Ms. Okeke's enthusiastic help, Izzy found several excellent articles to show Mr. Delmonico. "I think this one's the best," said Izzy. She showed Ms. Okeke an article about a team of girls who called themselves "the Hoppers."

Sixth-Grade Girls Win STEM Contest

The seven sixth-grade girls call their STEM team "the Hoppers" in honor of Grace Hopper, a computer pioneer. The Hoppers invented a compost receptacle that's biodegradable. They won their regional STEM tournament and their state tournament, and then they went to the World Finals and competed against kids from 25 countries. Every team was allowed only $145 for all their materials.

"Only a hundred and forty-five dollars for materials," said Ms. Okeke. "*That* should help Mr. Delmonico feel better about the budget."

Izzy printed copies of the newspaper articles they had found. She attached the STEM Team sign-up sheet to it. Then she wrote a note and attached it to the articles, too:

Dear Mr. Delmonico,

I'm Izzy Newton, the girl who suggested a STEM team here at Atom Middle School. You asked me to present you with research to share with the school board to convince them to approve the idea. Here it is. Ms. Okeke helped me.

I've attached the sign-up sheet. You can see that 24 students wrote their names on it to show their interest. I think even more kids would join the STEM team once it got started.

A STEM team would be fun, educational, and inexpensive. We could go to competitions, and we might also be able to solve problems right here at Atom Middle School. That way, we'd be following your One School Rule: Be kind.

Sincerely,

Isabelle Newton

Ms. Okeke gave Izzy a big manila envelope to put everything in. "Good luck, Ms. Newton," she said. "I'm rooting for you and your STEM team idea."

"Thanks!" said Izzy. "And thanks for all your help."

Izzy held the envelope close to her chest as she left the library.

"Hey," said Trevor, catching up to her. "What's that?"

"Stuff about STEM team," said Izzy.

"Good!" said Trevor. He gave Izzy a thumbs-up before he loped off down the hall to his locker.

Izzy walked to the principal's office. Mr. Delmonico was not there and the door to his office was closed, so Izzy slid the envelope under his door, where he'd be sure to see it first thing Monday morning. Izzy shivered. It was as chilly in the doorway outside Mr. Delmonico's office as it was in the rest of the school. *When we have a STEM team,* she thought, *WE'LL solve the mystery of the cold school!*

Izzy had finished her after-school task, so she went outside to watch the track team tryouts. Izzy sat in the sunniest spot on the bleachers to warm up. She was just in time to see a race with both Charlie and the new girl, Marie's friend, in the lineup.

Marie's friend had changed out of her school outfit and was wearing red tights underneath cut-off jeans, a T-shirt that said "Daytona Beach," a plaid shirt tied around her waist, purple high-tops, and brown socks. Her outfit looked like it had been collected from four different secondhand stores and thrown together any which way. But the new girl looked confident and completely comfortable—actually, *very* happy—not to look quite like anyone else. She didn't *look* mean. But Izzy frowned to herself when she recalled how snarky the new girl had been when she made fun of Izzy in the Girls' Room.

Breet! went the coach's whistle, and the runners were off.

Charlie ran so gracefully and effortlessly, her long legs stretching forward, that Izzy didn't realize how fast she was moving until she pulled out ahead of all the other runners. It was as if Charlie was not in a race at all but was just running by herself for the sheer pleasure of it. As Izzy watched Charlie run, she had a thought she'd had many times before: Charlie running was what beautiful music would look like if it were visible.

Izzy saw the new girl put on a burst of speed, her

plaid shirt flapping behind her. She nearly caught up
with Charlie. Charlie won, but only by a stride. The rest
of the runners cheered for her and thumped her on
the back after crossing the finish line themselves.
All except one: Marie's friend. She frowned, put her
hands on her hips, and walked away to catch her breath—
but also to avoid congratulating Charlie, Izzy was sure.

Nice new friend you've got there, Marie, thought Izzy.
She's snarky AND a sore loser!

"TGIF!" hollered Allie. She came flying up to Izzy and Charlie at their lockers after Charlie's practice. "Want to hang out?"

"Yes, but not at my house," said Izzy, pulling the books she needed for weekend homework out of her locker, "because we'll be interrupted nonstop. My brothers will bug you to play video games with them. It *kills* them that you always win."

"Just naturally brilliant, I guess." Allie shrugged, beaming. "What can I say?"

"I think your brothers are nice," said Charlie.

"They can be," said Izzy. She actually did have lots of fun with her brothers.

"And as I've told you a million times, your brothers are total eye candy," said Allie. "Definitely crush material."

"*Hunh,*" scoffed Izzy, rolling her eyes. "Talk about crush. They can *crush* about a million pancakes at breakfast, no sweat."

"*Ohh,*" moaned Charlie. "Pancakes! You're making me hungry. Let's go to my house. It's closest."

"Great!" said Izzy and Allie. They always liked to go to Charlie's. She and her moms and brothers lived in a big rambling old house. Charlie's moms were both veterinarians, so there were sometimes recuperating animals in the house, and just born baby animals to play with.

As they biked from school to Charlie's house, Allie asked, "So how'd it go with your STEM research, Izzy?"

"Easy-peasy," said Izzy. "Ms. Okeke and I found lots of good info."

"Did Mr. Delmonico agree to ask the board for money?" asked Charlie.

"Not yet," said Izzy. "He wasn't in his office, so I left my research and the sign-up sheet and a note in an envelope under his door. I hope we'll hear back from him soon. Maybe Monday."

"I've got my fingers crossed," said Charlie.

"It's so chilly out that my fingers have frozen around the handlebars of my bike!" joked Izzy. "Otherwise, I'd cross my fingers, too."

"A STEM team is an awesome idea," said Allie. "*Everybody* thinks so."

"I'm not so sure about that," said Izzy. "Some people think it's stupid."

"What do you mean?" asked Charlie. "Who thinks that a STEM team is stupid?"

"Well," said Izzy reluctantly. "You know Marie's friend, the one you just beat in a race?"

"Her name is Gina Carver," said Charlie.

"When I was in the Girls' Room," said Izzy, "I overheard Gina telling Marie that I was 'out there.' She said I was 'toxic' for liking ice hockey and suggesting a STEM team."

"'Toxic'?" repeated Charlie. She slammed on the brakes of her bike. Izzy and Allie stopped, too. "That's just plain wrong. *I* thought you were really brave for standing up for a STEM team. You *owned* it. And I know you hate being the center of attention."

"Yes!" agreed Allie loyally, as the girls started pedaling again. "You talked in front of *everybody,* Izzy, just like a regular person."

Izzy shuddered at the memory of the lunchroom on Thursday. She could hardly believe she'd been so brave herself! People who were not shy had no idea how excruciating it was for her to speak in front of people. And now it seemed that it was all for nothing. "I heard Gina talking Marie out of joining anything as uncool as a STEM team," she said. "And the three of us being on it is the kiss of death."

"It all adds up," said Allie. "Didn't I tell you Marie has dumped us? We're history now. So Marie's all palsy-walsy with that new hipster girl Gina—"

"What's a 'hipster'?" interrupted Izzy.

"Hipsters are ultracool and into retro stuff, like Gina's thrift-store outfit," said Allie. "It makes sense that Marie would glom on to a hipster. She's all about that 'I'm awesome without trying too hard' vibe."

"Well, upcycled clothing is super Earth-friendly," said Charlie. "I don't know … I was pretty impressed with Gina. She is *fast*. I only beat her by an eyelash today. And I like how she has lots of pockets on her clothes, like she's a marsupial."

"But Gina said mean stuff about Izzy," Allie said to Charlie. She turned to Izzy and said, "I think Marie is awful for not sticking up for you when Gina dissed you, Izzy." She shook her head and frowned. "Very lame."

Charlie said thoughtfully, "I think Marie is hiding something. But I guess we'll never know *what*. It's just going to be off-the-charts awkward, every time we meet up."

"Don't worry. We'll be like skew lines," said Allie, who liked to use ideas from math to explain things. "We'll pass each other, but our paths will never intersect, not ever, not even to infinity."

"I just wish I knew what we did that was so wrong," sighed Izzy.

The girls leaned their bikes against Charlie's house and headed inside.

"I don't think it's anything we did," Charlie said. "It's what we *are* in Marie's mind."

"Absolute zeros, coolness-wise, you mean?" said Izzy, shedding her jacket, hat, and scarf, grateful for the warmth in the kitchen.

Charlie nodded. "Marie thinks that if she's friends with us, we'll pull her coolness quotient down to rock-bottom because ours is so low."

"*Hey!* Speak for yourselves!" protested Allie. She swung her scarf around as if it was a feather boa and joked, "*Moi*, not cool? No way! What is middle school, an alternate universe?"

"The question is," said Izzy, getting to the heart of the matter, "what are we going to *do*? I refuse to just give up on being friends with Marie."

"Do you have a plan?" Charlie asked.

"Well," said Izzy. "Maybe somehow we could change Marie's mind."

"By changing *ourselves*?" asked Allie indignantly.

"No," said Izzy slowly and thoughtfully, "by changing something else, something … *important*."

"Like what?" asked Allie.

"Uh-oh, Allie! Red alert!" joked Charlie. "Man your battle stations: Izzy's got that 'I've got an idea' look. Run for cover!"

Allie laughed, but Izzy ignored Charlie. "What if," Izzy said, "we put our brains together and secretly, without telling anyone what we're doing until we're successful, solve the mystery of why the school is so cold?"

"Or maybe we could fix the problem of the crowded staircases," suggested Allie.

"Those are both good ideas," said Charlie. "We've put up with being frozen and crushed for three days solid. If the grown-ups were going to solve these problems, they would have done it by now."

"WE'LL do it! And every kid in the whole school will

love us!" said Allie. Her brain had a tendency to fast-forward through the tough parts of a challenge and go straight to the triumphs.

"We'd go from Absolute Zeros to Absolute Heroes," agreed Izzy. "We'd be doing Mr. Delmonico an act of kindness, too."

"That poor guy!" agreed Allie. "He *needs* kindness."

"And well, maybe, just maybe," Izzy said, "solving one of the mysteries would impress Marie and make her remember why she used to like us."

"Because we're math and science nerds?" asked Allie.

"I'm not sure whether she'll like us because of that or in spite of that," said Charlie, shaking her head.

"I'm all in on your idea, Iz!" said Allie, already raring to go. "Where do we start?"

"We start where we are," said Izzy, echoing Granddad. "That's usually best. So, I'll begin. I think the coldness problem is The Worst."

"I'll say!" said Allie. "It's *super* annoying! It's the coldest September ever, like a second Ice Age! And our school's heat doesn't work. The cold school is even more annoying than the stair jam. It's a drag having after-school activities canceled because the building is so cold that it's a safety hazard."

"My experiment in biology didn't even work because the fluids had a thin coating of ice on them," Charlie complained.

"You think that's bad," said Allie. "I couldn't feel my pencil in my hand in Math class. My hand was so cold it was *numb*."

Izzy laughed. "Okay, okay ... enough!" she said. "So, let's focus on the coldness problem. It's the one that we have the best chance of fixing. We just have to figure out why the air-conditioning keeps going *on* and the furnace keeps going *off*. It seems like first, we should go look at the thermostat. It controls the heat and air-conditioning going on and off."

"Where's the thermostat?" asked Allie.

"It's in the principal's office," said Izzy. "Remember? Mr. Delmonico mentioned it at the first-day assembly."

"There's only *one* thermostat for the whole school?" asked Allie.

Izzy shrugged. "It's an old building," she said. "I bet it didn't even *have* air-conditioning when it was first built."

"Okay, so, we go to—" Charlie began.

Just then, Charlie's little twin brothers, Caleb and Ben, ran in. "Charlie, Izzy, Allie!" they said. "Come see!" Caleb and Ben pulled the girls by their hands and dragged them back outside. Charlie's moms, Susannah and Laurie, were there, kneeling next to a big box by a shed.

"Puppies!" said Caleb, Ben, Charlie, Allie, and Izzy all together.

Charlie's moms laughed. "Someone dropped these puppies off at the animal hospital today," said Susannah. "You can look, but better not touch them because they haven't had their shots yet. *Ten cuidado.*"

"*Sí, Mami,*" said Charlie.

"They're golden retrievers," said Laurie, "about six weeks old. They need homes."

"Oh, I'd take them ALL," said Allie. "But my own dogs, Mimi and Mitzvah, would be jealous."

"I don't think Wickins would like a puppy, either," said Izzy sadly. "Though he's so lazy that he might not even notice."

"Look how they're all squished together," said Charlie. "It's so *cute*."

"They're adorable," agreed Izzy. "But they're so crowded they remind me of us in the halls, trying to get to Math class on time."

"The puppies cuddle to stay warm," said Laurie.

"*There's* an idea!" joked Izzy.

Susannah and Laurie looked surprised when the girls all laughed. So Charlie explained, "Remember how I told you that our school building is freezing? Well, we're going

to secretly try to figure out how to warm everybody up."

"Good for you!" said Susannah.

"Be sensible," said Laurie. "Don't do anything dangerous."

"Let's try to go look at the thermostat first thing Monday morning," said Izzy. "That'll be a safe and sensible place to start."

Charlie laughed. "Maybe we are as weird as Marie and her friend Gina think we are. Who else would voluntarily go to the principal's office? That's where you go when you're in trouble!"

Trouble? thought Izzy, suddenly anxious. *Is that what I'm leading us into?*

6

"Whoa!" breathed Izzy. Allie and Charlie bumped into her as she stopped short at the door of the principal's office Monday morning. "*This* is a surprise."

Izzy leaned back so Allie and Charlie could see past her. They gasped when they peeked through the open door and saw who was speaking to the principal: Marie and Gina!

"Maybe they're here to put their phones in phone jail," whispered Izzy.

"Yeah, a girl in my English class forgot to turn in her phone, and she got in trouble," said Allie.

Charlie watched the girls carefully. She was really good at reading body language and facial expressions. "Marie looks super serious," she said. "And Gina looks like she's ready for a fight."

Then the girls heard the principal say something that seemed to confirm that Marie and Gina were in hot water.

"All right," Mr. Delmonico said to Marie and Gina firmly. "One chance, girls. That's all I'm giving you. I'll walk you to class now, to be sure you get there on time."

"*Yikes*. Did they skip class on Friday?" whispered Allie.

Izzy's soft heart went out to Marie. She tried to smile at Marie as she and Gina left with Mr. Delmonico. But Marie rushed past without making eye contact, walking so swiftly that her phosphorescent sneakers made a glowing flash of color.

Izzy shivered. "Absolute zero," she sighed.

"Yes, it's *still* so cold in here!" agreed Charlie.

Izzy didn't contradict Charlie even though the temperature of the building wasn't really what Izzy was referring to.

Just after Mr. Delmonico left with Marie and Gina, a team of mechanics came out of the office. Izzy was too shy to approach them, but outgoing Allie bounced up to a technician and asked, "Why don't you just turn off the whole heating and air-conditioning system?"

"We did that," said the technician. "But it's so cold outside that the school got too cold inside. And no matter how cold it is inside, when we turn the system on, the air-conditioning goes on, not the heat."

"Bummer!" said Allie.

"You can say that again, kid!" said the technician.

When Izzy, Allie, and Charlie sneaked a peek into Mr. Delmonico's office, Izzy was glad to see that the manila envelope she'd left there Friday was on his desk but disappointed to see that it was sitting unopened atop a messy pile of papers.

"There's the thermostat," said Izzy, pointing. The thermostat was on the wall, just above a lamp that sat on the principal's desk. Sunlight streamed in through the window.

"Why is Mr. Delmonico wasting electricity by having his desk lamp turned on?" said Charlie, frowning. "It's a sunny day!"

"See where his chair is?" said Allie. "He's got his back to the window, so his shadow is cast over the desk. He has to have his light on even when it's sunny so he can see stuff clearly."

"Sunny! Aha!" said Izzy happily. "The sun! Are you guys thinking what I'm thinking?"

"I bet we are," said Charlie. "The sun shines straight onto the thermostat, so the thermostat thinks the temperature is hot, and the air-conditioning goes on."

Izzy nodded. "Our first—and, if we're right, *final*—hypothesis!" she said.

The three girls exchanged enthusiastic fist bumps. But they didn't have time to talk. They had to hurry off to their first classes.

In Math, Trevor poked Izzy in the back. "Hey," he said. "Any news from Mr. Delmonico?"

Izzy shook her head. "I don't think he's even opened the envelope yet," she said.

"Shoot," said Trevor. "Well, no news is good, right?"

"Not exactly," said Izzy. "It's more like inert."

When Izzy, Allie, and Charlie met at lunch, Allie said, "I thought for sure those repair people we saw in the principal's office would figure out the problem. But it doesn't feel like it. The school's still cold."

"So we haven't missed our chance to solve the Mystery of the Cold School," said Charlie, biting into a sub sandwich the size of a real submarine.

"We better be quick about it," said Allie.

"No," said Izzy firmly. "We have to be *scientific* about it. I've got it all planned." She pulled a black-and-white marble composition book out of her backpack. "I brought this for us. We'll keep a record of every single solitary step we take," she said. "Right now, I'll write our hypothesis about the thermostat."

"Oh, Izzy," sighed Allie. "Congratulations. You just won the Nerd of the Century Award. You are unbelievably c-a-r-e-f-u-l."

"Yup!" said Izzy cheerfully. She wrote the steps in the Scientific Method and their findings so far:

- Make an Observation: The school is too cold.
- Form a Question: Why is the air-conditioning/ heating system malfunctioning?
- Form a Hypothesis: The thermostat registers high temperatures because it is located in direct sunlight.
- Conduct an Experiment: Observe what happens when there is no sunlight shining on the thermostat.

"Okay, now we just have to wait for bad weather, and—" Allie began, but Charlie corrected her.

"There's no such thing as good or bad weather," said Charlie. "Nature needs rain and cold as much as it needs sun and heat."

"Okay, Ranger Rick!" said Allie, raising both hands in surrender.

"Anyway," said Izzy, "scientists have to use words that are more specific than 'good' or 'bad.' Today is 'sunny, warm, and dry' so we have to wait for a 'dark, cold, and rainy' day before we can go to the final step, which is …" Izzy said aloud as she wrote:

Analyze the Data and Draw a Conclusion

The girls were so absorbed in their plans that they lingered in the cafeteria too long and had to push their way through crowds of kids rushing to class in the tightly packed hallways.

"Just wait," said Izzy cheerfully. "When we figure out how to warm this place up, kids won't have to wear their bulky jackets anymore. That will free up so much space that it'll seem like the halls have magically gotten wider."

"Can't happen a moment too soon for me!" wailed

Allie, squashed between two tall eighth graders in giant ski parkas. "I'm tired of being the turkey in the middle of a middle-school sandwich!"

That evening, after dinner, Granddad sat next to Izzy on the couch and looked over her shoulder as she was trying to do her Forensics homework.

"Blank page, eh?" he asked.

Izzy sighed deeply. "I'm supposed to come up with a topic I want to make a speech about," she said. "And the problem is, I don't want to make a speech at all. About anything. Ever."

"Didn't you just tell me that you stood up in the cafeteria and spoke about a STEM team?" Granddad asked.

"Yes, but that just about did me in!" wailed Izzy. "And anyway, that wasn't a speech. That was one sentence that took five seconds, max. The idea of making a *real* speech is …" Izzy trailed off and then shook her head. "Right now, just *thinking* about it, my stomach's churning, my head's spinning, and my hands are shaky."

"You've got the Paper Due Flu," said Granddad. "I've seen the symptoms before, with your brothers. There's only one cure."

"What is it?" Izzy asked.

Instead of answering, Granddad asked, "Did I ever tell you about Sir Isaac Newton's first law? It says that 'An object at rest stays at rest and an object in motion stays in motion.'"

"I don't get it," said Izzy. "That doesn't have anything to do with me and my speech."

"Oh," said Granddad. "I think it does. Because loosely translated, in your case, Newton's first law means: Quit moping. Get moving."

Izzy had to laugh. "Very scientific!" she said.

Granddad nodded. "Newton's laws have many practical applications," he said as he stood. "I'll leave you to it."

But despite Granddad's advice, Izzy's page—and mind—remained empty of speech topics. And the next day, to add to Izzy's misery, the sky was a dismal gray. A chilling, weepy rain drizzled down. As the Atom Middle School students trudged into the building—bundled up, shuffling along in their boots and scarves and hats and gloves—Izzy heard complaints from every side:

"Now it's monsoon season!" muttered a boy.

"This is cruel and unusual punishment," complained an eighth-grade girl.

"I feel like I should be wearing waders," wailed another girl, "because it's so wet in here!"

"I'm calling Health and Human Services to complain!" shouted a boy, raising his arms over his head, fists clenched.

Yet another team of workers had dismantled the halls' overhead pipes, and students were hopping around an obstacle course of ladders and orange safety cones. Soon the floors were sloppy and slippery from the rain dripping off kids' coats and boots, which made the hallways slick underfoot. Izzy, Allie, and Charlie carefully wended their way to their lockers to put their books and lunches away.

"The school should hand out free hot chocolate," said Charlie, "to defrost us."

"Yeah, and, Izzy, you can play ice hockey right here in the hallway," joked Allie as she shut her locker door. "These puddles'll freeze any second now."

As she and Charlie laughed at Allie's joke, Izzy saw that Gina was passing their lockers. Gina was walking very quickly, bent forward as if she were eager to be the first student to reach the stairs. Suddenly, right by Allie's locker, Gina slid on the treacherous wet floor and lost her balance.

"Careful!" cried Allie. She reached out to steady Gina, but when she grabbed Gina's arm, Gina's water bottle fell out of her hand and onto the floor with a *clang*. Then it rolled away down the hall and was kicked, tripped over, and soon hopelessly lost in the tangle of students' feet.

Gina wrenched her arm free and frowned at Allie. "Thanks," she said sarcastically.

"Sorry," Allie apologized. "It was an accident."

"I bet," said Gina. "No wonder Marie told me your nickname is Allie *Oops*."

"Not '*oops*,' " Allie began. "Just one 'oop.' And I said I was sorry! You—"

But Gina rushed away before Allie finished.

Izzy, Charlie, and Allie looked at each other in dismay.

"*That* went well," said Allie, obviously meaning the opposite.

Suddenly, a deafening roar rocked the school. Students were clapping, stamping their feet, and cheering:

Cool!

Oh, man!

Wow!

Rad!

Totally, totally cool!

"What is it?" asked Izzy.

She and Charlie and Allie followed the crowd, and then they saw why everyone was cheering: The entire stairwell was ablaze with lights. Someone had taped strings of icicle lights to the wall. On the staircase to the left, the tiny bulbs lit one after another in a series that dripped down.

Behind the lights, there were huge arrows pointing down that were painted on long sheets of poster paper. On the staircase to the right, huge painted arrows pointed up, and icicle lights lit one after another in a series going up.

Izzy beamed. "An 'Up' staircase and a 'Down' staircase, with lights and arrows to remind us without words," she said. "Oh, this is The Best."

"Somebody beat us to fixing the stair problem," said Allie.

"Yeah, but I've never been gladder to be beaten in a race," said Charlie. "Whoever did this is brilliant."

"I know who did it," said Izzy.

"Who?" gasped Charlie and Allie. "How do you know?"

Izzy pointed toward the painted arrows. "That's phosphorescent paint," she said.

"Like on Marie's shoes!" said Allie.

Izzy nodded.

"Ahhh, so *that's* what the principal was saying to Marie and Gina," said Charlie. "He was giving them permission, but just *one* chance, to solve the staircase problem."

"Their plan's really working, too," said Izzy. "Everyone is going up one staircase and down the other. Come on! Let's follow the lights!"

Going up the illuminated stairs was fun, even though when she reached the top, Izzy had to go to Forensics. Luckily, Ms. Martinez asked students to stand and state their speech topics in alphabetical order according to the first letter of their last names. They got only as far as Amin Farud. Izzy figured if the recitations continued at that pace, she'd be able to slide under the radar on Thursday, too. She'd have all weekend and next Monday to think up a topic before they got as far as "N."

Later at lunch, Izzy said, "Marie is a genius, isn't she? We should ask her to help us with the cold school problem."

"Why bother?" said Charlie, pouring kombucha tea—a green liquid that looked like algae—out of her thermos and into her cup. "It's not like you to ignore all the evidence, Izzy. And all the evidence indicates that she'll say no. Asking her will be a flop."

"Speaking of flops," said Allie. "It looks—and *feels*—like our hypothesis about the thermostat is a flop, too." She turned on her tablet to show Izzy and Charlie her results. "I put a wireless thermometer in my locker and connected it to the Wi-Fi. Then I made up a program—"

"Way to go, Allie!" Izzy interrupted happily. "Looks like all that practice with computer games paid off!"

"Totally," said Allie. "As I was saying, I made up a program to track the temperature of the school building, and my data show that the problem doesn't go away when it's dark, rainy, cloudy, and sunless like it is today. So heat from the sun shining on the thermostat is NOT the cause of the air-conditioning problem."

"Who needs a computer program?" asked Charlie. "My numb fingers tell me the same thing." She used her homemade pretzel stick to point first to her eyes and then to her free hand. "I can *see* that it's gray and rainy and I can *feel* that the air-conditioning is on. That means the sun isn't fooling the thermostat. Something else must be making it all wonky." She bit off the end of her pretzel and sighed with discouragement as she concluded, "That shoots our hypothesis down."

"It's only our *first* hypothesis," said Izzy. "I'll record our results." She completed the entry:

- Make an Observation: The school is too cold.
- Form a Question: Why is the air-conditioning/ heating system malfunctioning?
- Form a Hypothesis: The thermostat registers high temperatures because it is located in direct sunlight.

- Conduct an Experiment: Observe what happens when there is no sunlight shining on the thermostat.
- Analyze the Data and Draw a Conclusion: Even on a gray, rainy day with no sunshine, the air conditioner is on, so the sun is NOT fooling the thermostat.

Allie looked over her shoulder and heaved a big sigh.

"Never mind," said Izzy. "Don't get all bummed out yet. I've already thought of another hypothesis."

Allie and Charlie burst out laughing.

"What's so funny?" asked Izzy.

"*You* are!" said Allie. "Once you get going, you're like a steam engine or something. You're unstoppable."

"Well," said Izzy, laughing now, too. "I'm just like Newton's first law: 'An object at rest stays at rest and an object in motion stays in motion.' So here's what I need you to do, Allie. Can you look online for some aerial photos of the school building? Then we can see what section of the roof the air-conditioner condenser and exhaust fans are on."

It took Allie only a second to find satellite photos of

the school on her tablet and zoom in on the condensers and fans on the roof above the auditorium.

"But I don't get it," said Charlie. "What good does this photo do us?"

"The air-conditioning units could be broken and the reason for all these problems," Izzy replied.

"But wouldn't the repair people have figured that out already?" Charlie asked.

"Well, if they did figure it out, they obviously didn't fix it because it's still freezing in this building," said Allie.

"We can't get to the AC stuff on the *roof*!" said Charlie.

Izzy tilted her head and raised her eyebrows.

"Oh no," said Charlie, "you're not thinking that we'll somehow climb out onto the roof?"

"You're the athlete," said Allie. "Why are you being such a wimp?"

"I'm not," said Charlie. "I'm just being safe and sensible, like my mom told us to be."

"Well, don't worry. We don't exactly have to *climb* out onto the roof," reassured Izzy. "When we had our assembly in the auditorium, I noticed that there was a metal staircase at the back of the stage. I think it leads up to the catwalks. I bet from there we could find stairs up to the roof."

"Let's go!" said Allie, leaping to her feet.

"No!" said Charlie, thumping her thermos on the table.

Izzy and Allie both jumped at the noise.

"Charlie is right," said Izzy. "We'd better wait until we have more time and also wait until the school is empty."

"That's not what I meant," said Charlie. "I meant that this is *not* a good idea! But what's the use?" She shook her head and said, half-joking, "Izzy Newton's in motion and there's no stopping her."

A businesslike wind had blown the rain and clouds away later that afternoon. After the last late bus had left, Izzy, Allie, and Charlie met at their lockers. They headed to the auditorium and, looking back to make sure they weren't seen, slipped backstage.

"Follow me," whispered Izzy. The three girls walked past the dressing rooms and up a dark, winding staircase, their footsteps clanging on the metal. They inched their way, heel-toe-heel-toe, along the catwalks high above the stage, climbed up a steep wooden ladder, and found a small room. There was a skylight, but it was so dirt-encrusted that only a little sun came through, so the room was dark until Charlie flicked the light switch to ON. The girls saw some dusty, old-looking boxes slumped against each other in the corners.

"Look," said Izzy, pointing. "I bet that door leads out to the roof."

"Careful! It'll be slippery out there," warned Charlie as Izzy groped in the dark for the door handle.

With a *whoosh,* Izzy pushed the door open and stepped outside.

"Holy moly!" exclaimed Allie, right behind her. "Wow!"

"Isn't this The Best?" breathed Izzy.

"It sure is," said Charlie, joining them, "especially on such a gorgeous, windy day."

The wind whistled through the girls' clothes, swirled their hair, and made their eyes water. "The wind's so strong it feels as though it could lift me up into the sky," said Izzy, enraptured.

"Sweet," said Charlie.

The girls were so exhilarated to be up high that they explored the roof and looked at the view from every direction, forgetting momentarily to inspect the air-conditioner condenser and fans. The roof was flat, covered in tar paper, and there were puddles clogged with clumps of leaves here and there where the roof had sunk in a bit. Izzy saw some collapsed wooden boxes and what looked like abandoned tools. Altogether, the roof looked rather neglected, as if no one went up there very often.

"You know," said Izzy eagerly. "I think we've discovered something. I think we've found a secret hangout for ourselves to go to when we want to get away from the noise and the crowds."

"Yes!" agreed Allie. "If it's raining, we could hang out

in that little room we came through just now. We could decorate it—or at least bring pillows to sit on, and maybe some lamps."

"We could keep a supply of snacks there!" said Charlie. "And when the weather is nice, we could meet out here on the roof and have picnics. We could have bird feeders and plant grass out here, and have a little garden to grow carrots, or maybe strawberries."

"It looks like someone already HAD a garden up here a long time ago," said Allie, pointing to plant boxes with old, dead stems and leaves in them. "Am I paranoid after the lake, or is that poison ivy? And look! *Bees!* They're just lying there, but some of them are still alive."

"Bees don't die until their body temperature is forty-one degrees," said Charlie. "I know, because my moms keep beehives. But bees can't fly when the air temperature is below fifty-five degrees, and it's definitely colder than that today. This is such weird weather for September!"

"Okay, okay! Enough bee facts!" said Allie. She shuddered. "Even these zombie bees scare me. What if they wake up mad? Come on. Let's get to work. Let's look at the air conditioners and stuff."

As they walked across the roof, Izzy enthused, "We could have wind turbines, and maybe a telescope for stargazing, and a weather tracking station, and—"

All of a sudden, there was a huge gust of wind.

BAM!

The one door that led back inside slammed shut so hard that it seemed like it would never open again.

8

"Oh, no!" cried Izzy. She, Allie, and Charlie tugged on the door handle while the wind whipped their hair into their eyes. But the door was stuck shut. It would not open, no matter how hard the girls pulled.

"Help!" all three girls yelled—at the door, at the sky, over the edge of the building—even though they knew that yelling was useless. The wind blew their words away, and besides, everyone had left for the day. There was no one around to hear their cries for help.

The girls huddled in the shelter of the doorway, out of the wind.

"What are we going to do?" asked Allie, panic rising in her voice. "We could be stuck here all night!"

"We'll starve to death," moaned Charlie. She was

always calm unless food-deprived. "Maybe those bees made a honeycomb somewhere up here. I'm *already* getting weak from hunger."

"I'm sure there's a way down," said Izzy, with more hope than certainty. "Let's look for a ladder."

The girls fanned out and searched the rooftop. When they met up again, no one had located a ladder, but Charlie had found a hose. "We can loop this around one of the air-conditioner condensers," she said. "And I'll shimmy down to the ground."

"Wait!" said Izzy. Her heart was thumping, and she could hardly believe what she heard her own voice saying, "I'm the littlest and lightest, so I think I should be the one to shimmy down."

"Are you sure?" asked Charlie.

Izzy grinned. "No, I'm not at all sure," she admitted. "I'm scared stiff. But you are by far the strongest one of us, so it'll be best for you to stay here and hold on to the end of the hose, right?"

Charlie only nodded, but Allie said helpfully, "Pretend it's the rope swing at the lake. Just remember you're over land and not water."

All three girls burst out into nervous laughter. Then they got to work. And it was hard work, too: The hose was very dirty and very heavy, so it was cumbersome work to haul it over to the air-conditioner condenser, uncoil part of it, wind a few loops around the condenser, and then drag and drop the rest of it over the edge of the roof.

Charlie and Allie braced their feet against the condenser and took a firm hold on their end of the hose. Izzy, whose arms were already tired and achy from wrestling with the hose, went to the edge of the roof and turned to face Charlie and Allie. She straddled the hose, grabbed it in both trembling hands, and called out, "Bye!"

"Be careful, Izzy," cautioned Charlie.

"Hold on tight," added Allie.

Tentatively, Izzy lowered herself over the edge of the roof. *This is the stupidest thing I have ever done,* she thought. But she had no choice.

The hose was slick and cold, so she squeezed it between her knees and twisted it around her feet for extra grip. The wind blew her so hard against the bricks of the building that she bounced against them, as if she were rappelling down a rock face. Inch by inch at first, she slid down the

hose. She soon realized that she was holding on with too much tension and that if she relaxed her grip her shoulders and legs wouldn't cramp up and she'd slide more easily. Her pants and jacket were already streaked with dirt, and her hands and face were, too, because she was hugging the hose so closely. A sudden gust thrust her hard against the building, and the impact made her shoulder hurt so much that she yelped. But there was no going back and no stopping. There was only one thing to do: keep going. Izzy grinned to herself, thinking, *A body in motion* stays *in motion, right?*

Gingerly, Izzy lowered herself down the dangling rope past the windows of a second-floor classroom, hoping the wind wouldn't smack her against the glass hard enough to shatter it. She made it past safely. But there was no relief, because she was instantly dangling in front of the windows of a first-floor classroom.

Then the weirdest thing of all happened. Izzy looked in the windows and realized she was staring into the science lab—and staring back at her was *Marie.*

Izzy was so surprised that she lost her grip for a second and slid sickeningly out of control till she found a foothold on the outdoor windowsill. Marie, bundled up in her jacket in the cold classroom, was gaping at her, slack-jawed. All Izzy could do was smile a watery smile as she dropped the last few feet to the ground. Her hands were so clenched that it hurt to straighten her fingers. But the pain was nothing in comparison to the worry and confusion: *Marie isn't my friend anymore, so will she tell on me? What was Marie doing in the chemistry lab after school anyway? Why hadn't she gone home like everyone else?*

Izzy was certainly in no position to wait and wonder. She had to hit the ground running and race to free Allie and Charlie. She flew through the chilly school building and up the dark, twisty path to the little room that led to the roof. Izzy hurled herself at the door, and with all her strength, she forced it open.

Charlie and Allie had pulled the hose back up onto the roof, coiled it neatly, and put it back where they'd found it. Now they tumbled breathlessly inside. "Thank you," they gasped, hugging Izzy hard.

"Are you okay?" asked Charlie.

"How'd it go?" asked Allie.

"Fine," Izzy answered both questions quickly. "But we

may be in trouble."

"Now what?" asked Charlie.

Izzy struggled to catch her breath. "Marie saw me," she said.

"What?" gasped Charlie in disbelief.

"Oh, *noooo*," swooned Allie. "How?"

"Marie was in the science lab," Izzy explained. "And she saw me slide down the hose past the window."

"What are the chances?" asked Charlie. "Nine hundred students in this school, and the ONE kid who for some mysterious reason has a grudge against us catches Izzy in the act. That is bad luck."

"Come on," said Izzy. "We've got to go to the lab and try to talk to her."

"If she tells on us, we're toast," said Allie.

"Don't mention toast," said Charlie. "You're making my stomach growl."

They hurried to the science lab. But when they got there, Marie was gone. The room was cold and deserted.

"Do you think she'll rat us out?" asked Izzy. "She never used to be a tattler."

"Who knows?" said Charlie matter-of-factly. "Who

knows what Marie is or is not these days?"

"Oh, I think we know perfectly well what she is *not*," said Allie. "She is NOT our friend."

"We'll just have to wait and see what she'll do," said Izzy, sounding resigned.

"*Arrgghh*," moaned Allie dramatically. "Agony! I HATE to wait and see!"

Later that afternoon, the girls walked to Allie's apartment to do their homework together. Also, they were still shaken up and needed to talk.

"I need a big, whopping dose of chocolate, stat," said Charlie, "like some of those giant chocolate chip cookies that your grandmother makes, Allie. The ones that are more chocolate chip than cookie."

"Really, Miss Organic?" teased Allie. "You know Bubbie's cookies have all kinds of ingredients in them that don't grow in gardens."

"Desperate times call for desperate measures," said Charlie.

"Or in this case, desperate *pleasures*," joked Izzy. "And me too, by the way. I could really use a chocolate chip cookie, or maybe twenty. Bubbie's are—"

"The Best," Charlie chimed in with Izzy.

"Don't worry," said Allie. "Bubbie keeps a stash on hand at all times, in case of emergencies—like right now."

Allie lived with her grandmother Bubbie and her younger sister, Maja. Bubbie had been a world traveler and spoke lots of different languages and had friends all over the globe. But now she mostly took care of Allie and Maja, whom she called "the Grandgirls," because their mom was an archaeologist who was seldom home. Allie's mom Skyped and FaceTimed a lot, and she sent Allie and Maya cool stuff from wherever she was on a dig. But it was Bubbie who showered Allie and her friends with attention—and great snacks.

As the girls walked into Bubbie's painting studio, she said, "I have never seen three glummer faces in my life." She peered at the girls around the edge of her easel. "You look more sour than these lemons in the still life I'm painting. I'm not even going to speak to you until you've had a snack. Go to the kitchen and get some cookies."

"Thanks, Bubbie!" said all three girls. They dashed to the kitchen, grabbed as many cookies as they could hold, and returned to Bubbie.

As they chowed down, Bubbie asked, "Now, spill. What's the matter with you three?"

"We think we're in trouble," said Allie, straight out.

"What kind of trouble?" asked Bubbie.

"We're doing a science experiment, trying to fix something that's really important," said Izzy, "and we—I—

did something kind of dangerous and somebody saw me."

"Any broken bones or ruined property?" asked Bubbie.

"Well, no," said Izzy. "But maybe a broken rule or two."

"What did you *do*?" asked Bubbie.

"I slid down a hose," said Izzy, "from the roof of the school to the ground."

Bubbie grimaced. "Promise me you won't do *that* again," she said.

"I promise," said Izzy.

"Well," sighed Bubbie, "as long as no one and nothing was hurt and you promise you won't do any more death-defying stunts, I wouldn't worry too much. Sometimes rules have to be broken. You know what they say: 'Well-behaved women rarely make history.' You girls go ahead and be subversive. Just be careful, too." She went back behind her easel. "Now go to the kitchen and get yourselves more cookies, and maybe some juice this time. I've got to get back to work."

The evening was agonizingly long and full of anxiety for Izzy. When the girls rode their bikes to school on Wednesday morning, the wind was still cold and strong. It pushed against their backs, and Izzy had to fight the gnawing feeling that the wind was whisking her straight into trouble—or at the very least, into some sharp words from Mr. Delmonico. Would she be called to his office that day, after Marie had had a chance to squeal on her?

"Don't worry, Izzy," said Charlie kindly as they opened their lockers. They didn't take off their jackets because the school was still freezing. "Allie and I won't let you take all the blame. If Marie tells Mr. Delmonico that she saw you dangling outside the chemistry lab window, Allie and I will tell him we were on the roof, holding the other end of the hose."

"Of course!" agreed Allie. "We've got your back. Don't worry."

"Thanks," said Izzy. She wasn't completely reassured, but she was grateful to her loyal friends. She knew that conscientious Charlie didn't like to break rules or do anything that might seem unsportsmanlike. Even Allie, who usually didn't blink an eye at pushing limits, was nervous this morning.

Oh, if only I could talk to Marie! Izzy thought. But Izzy's only glimpse of Marie that morning was from afar; she was at the top of the Up staircase when Izzy was at the bottom. Marie wore a sparkly knit cap, and Izzy saw it glitter as the flecks caught the glow from the icicle lights in the stairwell.

The morning dragged by in slo-mo; it was as if time itself was as cold and sluggish as the students at Atom Middle School. The cold made some kids sleepy, and everyone's heavy jackets weighed them down so that they plodded like elephants from class to class.

When Mr. Delmonico hadn't summoned her by lunchtime, Izzy said to Allie and Charlie, "It looks like Marie didn't tell on us."

"Yet," added Allie ominously.

"Listen," said Izzy, her voice tight with tension. "Sitting around waiting is driving me crazy with worry. Let's *do* something. I really want to solve the mystery of why the school is so cold. The technicians clearly haven't fixed the problem, and I'm tired of shivering."

"Me too!" agreed Allie. "Also, I've worn all my best winter outfits already, about eight times each! And there's no way Bubbie will let me buy any new clothes, after I dyed all my back-to-school clothes blue."

Izzy and Charlie laughed sympathetically, which helped Izzy relax. She stood up. "Come on," she said. "Let's use the rest of lunchtime to go back up onto the roof and inspect the air-conditioner condenser and fan, like we were supposed to do yesterday."

"Okay," Charlie said, taking a last bite of tofu. "But this time, I'm going to prop the door open so we don't get stuck out there."

Hoping that no one was watching them, the girls followed the shadowy, serpentine path to the little room. When they came to the door that led outside, Charlie not only propped it open with a cement block, but she also tied a scarf around the handle so it couldn't automatically lock behind them. It turned out that all their trouble was for nothing anyway: They inspected the air-conditioner condensers and fans as well as they could without dismantling them, but it was clear that the machinery was working all too well. It hummed and whirred merrily.

"This is not where the problem is," said Izzy.

"We'll have to shoot THAT hypothesis down, too," said Allie, sounding frustrated.

As Izzy, Allie, and Charlie walked past the dressing rooms backstage on their way out, they heard a sound coming from the last door. *Someone was crying.*

9

Silently, Izzy pushed open the door to the dressing room and there was Marie, sobbing. She was all by herself, but her image was nightmarishly multiplied by the mirrors on the walls.

The girls stared at one another for a second, stunned wordless. Izzy saw that Marie's face was so dissolved in misery that at last it didn't have the pinched look it had had every time they'd seen her lately. Izzy's heart melted. She rushed to Marie and stood beside her, gently putting a hand on her shoulder. "What's the matter?" Izzy asked. "Are you hurt?"

"No!" Marie choked over her tears, but Izzy noticed that she didn't shrug off Izzy's comforting hand.

Izzy gave her a gentle squeeze. "Come on," she said.

"It's me, Izzy. Tell me what's wrong."

"I'm … fine … go away … leave me alone … all of you," Marie blurted out in between tearful hiccups.

"Marie, we're just trying to help," Izzy said.

"Help?" wailed Marie. "*Nothing* can help!"

"Blow your nose," said Charlie. "That'll help." She handed Marie a tissue, and Marie blew her nose really hard.

"Okay," said Izzy. "Now talk to us."

Marie gulped. "It's so *stupid*," she said. "Yesterday, Gina and I were babysitting my nephew, and we made slime. After, I thought we'd cleaned it all up. But he must have found some. Because this morning, I …" Marie's chin quivered, but she went on, "I pulled on this hat, and it was so cold in the building that I left it on all morning. And just now, when I tried to take it off, I couldn't. It's stuck on my hair! My nephew must have put a glob of slime in my hat, and …" Marie lifted the hat, and the girls saw that clumps of her hair were stuck together—and stuck to her knit hat—with globs of dried-up green slime. "Now I can't get the hat off. And how will I ever get the dried slime out of my hair?"

Izzy, Allie, and Charlie all talked at once:

Izzy said, "You have a nephew? And you and Gina made slime? Just like we used to?"

Allie said, "So that explains the hat! You weren't just trying to look French?"

And Charlie said, "Your hair looks bad now, but the slime will grow out eventually."

Marie nodded yes to Izzy's questions, shook her head no to Allie's, and said to Charlie, "But I'm supposed to have my school photo taken today. For the yearbook! For my ID! For everyone to see forever!"

"Wear your sparkly hat in the photo," suggested Allie.

"I don't even *like* this hat," said Marie. "I grabbed it in desperation when I left the house."

"Well then, I'll get scissors," said Allie. "We'll cut the hat off and then cut the slime out of your hair."

"Or we could cut all your hair as short as a crew cut," said Charlie, "so it looks like you want it that way."

"*Nooo,*" moaned Marie. "I'll be bald!"

"Not for long," soothed Charlie. "Hair grows at the rate of half an inch a month."

"So in a year, your hair will be six inches long," Allie

calculated cheerfully. "In two years, it'll be a foot long."

"Or maybe you could ask the photographer to Photoshop some hair onto your head," suggested Charlie.

"Stop," said Izzy, putting up her right palm. "Granddad and I are always getting stuff we're experimenting with stuck on our clothes or in our hair. We don't have to cut the slime out of Marie's hair. We'll freeze it, and then we'll be able to break it off in chunks. We'll need ice cubes, and then some lotion to get the dusty bits off her hair."

"Oh, thank you, Izzy!" said Marie. "I really didn't want to be bald. You're a genius!"

Izzy shrugged off Marie's compliment, but she was very pleased.

Charlie sprinted off to the cafeteria and was back in a jiffy with ice cubes—and olive oil.

"Really? Olive oil? Marie is going to smell like a salad," said Allie.

"It was either olive oil or peanut butter," said Charlie.

"Eww!" squealed all the girls at once at the idea of peanut-butter-scented hair. "Gross!"

"Yeah," agreed Charlie, "as much as I love peanut butter, the idea of Marie smelling like a sandwich seemed like a nonstarter."

"I'd say olive oil's better than peanut butter any day," joked Marie, "right off the top of my head."

The girls laughed. Izzy was so happy to hear Marie joking like the old days, she could have hugged her! Instead, she went to work on Marie's head. First, very gingerly, she lifted the sides of Marie's hat until the hat was inside out. Then, where it was still stuck, she cut the hat off Marie's hair. It was ruined, but Marie said, "I never want to see that hat again in my life!" Then Izzy held the ice against Marie's hair to freeze the slime.

While they waited for the slime to freeze, Izzy asked, "So, Marie, you said you were babysitting your nephew?"

"Yes, I babysit almost every afternoon," said Marie. "That's why I can't come to any of your houses after school. Crosby's a perpetual motion machine, and I have to watch him like a hawk. I promised that I wouldn't have anybody over because my mom and my sister think that I would be distracted if I did."

"But you invited that new girl Gina over," said Allie.

"Gina's Crosby's aunt, too, just like me," said Marie. "Gina's brother is married to my sister. So my mom doesn't mind if *she* comes over, just not anyone else who might be noisy or messy or anything."

"Oh, that sounds like she means *us*!" said Izzy. "I *knew* your mom never forgave us for that kitchen explosion!"

"But why didn't you tell us all this?" asked Charlie. "We would have understood."

"Yes," said Allie. "We thought you didn't want to be our friend anymore. We thought you thought we were absolute zeros."

"Well," Marie admitted, "I *was* mad at you! On the first day of school, all three of you rushed toward me acting like nothing had changed. You were all 'swish cheese sandwiches' and 'See you later, alligator.' It felt so fake!

I was awfully lonely at first in France, and you kept sending photos of all the fun you were having without me. Talk about feeling like a zero! I sure did."

"Oh, we didn't mean to make you feel left out!" said Izzy, stricken. "We wanted to show you how much we missed you."

"Then how come later on, when I sent you photos, you stopped sending any to me?" demanded Marie.

"You looked so different and sophisticated in the photos that we hardly recognized you," said Charlie. "Like, in the photos you sent after you got those haircuts, you looked so, I don't know, edgy and cool, like a rock star or something."

"And the photos that we sent you bounced back," explained Izzy.

"They did?" asked Marie. "But—"

"Hey!" said Allie. "By any chance, did you change your email address and forget to tell us, Marie?"

"Oh no! Maybe I did forget to tell you!" said Marie. "So *that's* what happened. But we could have cleared that up if you'd answered my phone call. I told you I'd call October 12."

"No, you wrote that you'd call on December 10," said

Charlie. "I remember because that's my dog's birthday, so we had cake. When you didn't call us, we tried to call you that day, but there was no answer."

Marie shook her head. "Oh," she sighed. She sounded embarrassed. "I bet I know what happened there, too, now that I think of it. In France, you write a date with the number of the day first, and then the month. So I wrote '12/10' and you thought I meant December 10, but I meant October 12."

The date mistake struck all the girls as hilariously silly, and they giggled hard. "I'm so glad the truth is revealed at last," said Izzy.

"Thanks for clearing things up, Marie," said Charlie.

"Yes," said Izzy. "And also, thank you for not telling on me when you saw me climbing down the hose. Why were you in the chemistry lab that afternoon after school?"

"I left my backpack in there by mistake," said Marie. She sighed. "I can NOT remember my locker combination, so I have to carry my backpack everywhere. It's a drag."

"I can help you remember your combination," said Allie. "What is it?"

"26-13-3," said Marie.

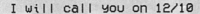

"Twenty-six letters in the alphabet," said Allie immediately. "The thirteenth is M, your first initial, and the third is C, your last initial."

"Allie, you are brilliant!" said Marie. "I'll never forget my locker combination again." She turned to Izzy. "Now it's my turn to ask *you*," she said. "Where were you coming from when I saw you shimmying down the hose?"

"We were all up on the roof," said Izzy.

"And the door slammed shut and we got stuck up there!" exclaimed Allie, shuddering at the memory of being marooned.

"We just about died of starvation," added Charlie.

"What were you doing on the *roof*?" asked Marie.

"We were supposed to be looking at the air-conditioner condenser and fan," said Charlie. "We want to figure out why the building is so cold."

"But we got kind of distracted by the view, and how nice it is on the roof, and then, *boom*. The door closed, and we freaked out," said Allie.

"Anyway, we were up there again just now," said Izzy, "and we *did* look at the machinery. Unfortunately, the condenser and fan do not seem to be the problem."

She took out the composition book. "I'm keeping a written record of our hypotheses."

Izzy wrote:

- Make an Observation: The school is too cold.
- Form a Question: Why is the air-conditioning/ heating system malfunctioning?
- Form a Hypothesis: The air-conditioner condenser and fan are malfunctioning.
- Conduct an Experiment: Observe the air-conditioner condenser and fan.
- Analyze the Data and Draw a Conclusion: Air-conditioner condensers and fans are working just fine. They are NOT the problem.

Allie threw up her hands, exasperated. "*Arrggh!* So now we're back to square one," she said.

"Oh," said Marie eagerly, "I'd like to help you solve that mystery. In fact, when I went back to the lab to get my backpack, I also was looking up Freon, the gas that's used in air-conditioning. But I guess you've proven that's not where the problem is."

"You're right," said Izzy.

"You know," said Marie, "I'll tell you who could be a big help to us: Gina. She's really smart. I bet she could make a sketch of the whole heating and air-conditioning system. She helped me when—" Marie stopped.

"Marie, your phosphorescent shoes gave you away!" said Izzy. "We know you're the one who came up with the great solution of the lights on the staircases. That was The Best. And it's great how you kept it a secret that *you* did it."

"Well, it was Gina's idea to use the lights AND the phosphorescent paint on the posters," said Marie. "Really, we'd BOTH like to help with the temperature problem."

Izzy, Allie, and Charlie exchanged glances, thinking of the conversation that Izzy had overheard in the Girls' Room between Marie and Gina.

"What's wrong?" asked Marie as she saw the looks on their faces.

Izzy spoke reluctantly. "I heard Gina say that she thought I was 'out there.'"

"Yes, that's right," said Marie. "She thinks you are awesome."

Izzy shook her head. "No, I heard her say I was '*toxic*.'"

"Yes, exactly. 'Toxic' is a high compliment in Gina-talk," said Marie. "She likes to flip words. You know, like when people say 'sick' when they mean 'great.' Gina thinks it's supercool how you like ice hockey and physics."

Izzy gave Marie a skeptical look.

"I'm serious, Izzy," said Marie. "You completely misunderstood Gina. Just wait until you meet her, you'll see. She's not mean."

"So then why does she keep giving Charlie and me serious side-eye every time we see her?" asked Allie.

"Gina's not used to losing," Marie explained. "She was mad at herself about that race. Every time she saw you, Charlie, it reminded her of her defeat. And she thinks *you* tripped her on purpose, Allie. But I told her that Charlie just *is* that fast and she'd better get used to it. And I told her that you'd never trip anybody, Allie, except maybe yourself over your own feet to get a laugh." Marie looked serious. "I think she would have changed her mind about you two, but all three of you shunned us."

"We thought *you* were shunning *us*!" squeaked Allie in protest.

"But we were wrong about you, too, Marie," said Charlie. "We thought that because you look different now, you must *be* different, too."

"But you're not," said Izzy happily. "You're still Marie. And thanks to the ice and oil, you're a slime-free Marie. Ta-da!"

"Thank you," said Marie. She smiled as she patted her hair and looked at herself in the mirror, saying, "Nice." Then she turned and hugged Izzy. "You've all got to hurry off to your afternoon classes right now. And *I* am going to have my school photo taken. I look okay, thanks to you guys. But Gina and I don't have to babysit for Crosby the Slime Baby today, so let's meet after your clubs end, okay?"

"Great!" said Izzy. "Let's meet here in the dressing room. We'll show you our secret hideout."

"Secret hideout?" repeated Marie. "*Fantastique!* Gina and I will meet up with you. Together maybe we can crack this case and turn up the heat in the school. Deal?"

"Deal!" said Izzy. She was so happy she felt as though she could fly.

10

Izzy had marching band practice after school that day. She knew she was playing "The Star-Spangled Banner" a beat ahead of everyone else; her flute sounded like audio on fast-forward. But she was so eager to meet up with Marie, Gina, Allie, and Charlie that she couldn't slow herself down.

Marie must have been excited, too, because she was already in the dressing room combing her hair when Izzy got there after band practice. Charlie and Gina arrived together after track practice. Gina seemed to have forgotten about losing the race. She and Charlie chatted animatedly about being on the relay team together while they shared a bag of carrots. Gina's brown eyes were magnified behind her thick-rimmed big glasses, and

instead of a kilt pin, her plaid skirt was held shut with a pin that said "VOTE."

Allie flew in late. "Here I am, here I am!" she said breathlessly.

Marie introduced Gina to Izzy and Allie, and then Allie said, "Sorry I'm late. I skipped out of Chess Club and the Homecoming Float Planning Committee meeting, but I was just elected president of the Math Club. I'm the first sixth grader *ever* elected president! So I couldn't leave *that* meeting early." Allie spoke to Charlie, Gina, and Marie. "By the way, have you guys met this kid named Trevor Gawande? He showed up at Math Club, and I just kept staring at him because, *whoa!*"

"Oh, I *know*," said Marie. "You'd love him, Izzy, because he's all about physics."

"Oh, ho, ho, step back! Izzy knows Trevor already," said Allie, bringing Marie up to speed. "He's in Math class with us. Anyway, I don't know about physics, but he's pretty sharp at math. Not scary smart, like Izzy and me, but close. And he's so cute! Don't you feel like you should observe a moment of silence in his honor when you see him?"

"Yes!" said Gina. "That boy is so cool, he's *ice*."

The girls laughed, and then Allie said, "Trevor asked me where *you* were, Izzy, and how come you're not in Math Club. I *told* you he has a crush on you."

"Oooo-ooo," cooed Marie, Gina, and Charlie.

"Don't be ridiculous," said Izzy briskly. She changed the subject ASAP. "Come on, Allie. We were just about to show Marie and Gina the roof."

Izzy led the single-file parade of Charlie, Gina, Marie, and Allie up the now familiar dark, winding staircase, along the narrow catwalks high above the stage, up the steep wooden ladder, and into the small room with the door that led out onto the roof. "This is the secret room we were telling you about," she said to Marie.

"I love it," said Marie.

"Isn't it wonderful?" said Charlie. "We are going to keep a cooler up here, for snacks."

"The room is nice," said Izzy. "But here's what *I* think is The Best." She leaned against the door to the roof and pushed it open. A gust of cold air rushed at the girls. Charlie very carefully propped the door open with the cement block and tied her scarf around the handle again so it couldn't lock them out.

"Oh, man!" said Gina. "This roof is awesome. You can see everywhere! Sky all around, like you're IN the sky."

Izzy said, "I was thinking that we should have a telescope up here and come look at the stars some night."

"Solid!" said Gina. "That would be sick!"

Marie raised her eyebrows and shared a grin with Izzy. "I love it up here," said Marie, "but the wind's wrecking my hair. Can we go back inside?"

Even indoors they felt windblown and chilled. Charlie shivered. "It feels like my core body temperature is dropping fast. We better solve this cold problem before hypothermia kicks in."

"Right," said Izzy. "And the more of us working on the problem, the merrier." She wanted to be very sure that Gina and Marie felt like they were part of the team, so she asked them, "What do you two think we should do?"

"Well, what have you guys done so far?" Gina asked, sounding very no-nonsense. "Give us a recap."

"Oh, before we talk about that I've just got to say, look at your cardigan! It's too cute!" gushed Allie.

"Thanks," said Gina. She wore a vintage cardigan decorated with tiny beads. "I think I've got a flyer about the secondhand store where I bought it." She dug down into her backpack, pulling out chopsticks, a hole punch, two LED light bulbs, paint chips, and a yo-yo.

"Gina, your bag is a disaster," teased Marie. "It's a mini version of your locker, which is a total nightmare."

"Well, I need stuff for my projects," said Gina. She handed Allie the flyer about the secondhand clothing store and then pulled a rhinestone tiara out of her pack. "You never know when you might need a tiara, for instance," she joked.

"Right!" everyone laughed.

"Gina, it'll be fun having you and Marie on our team," said Allie. Her face lit up. "Oh, oh, OH!" she exploded, flapping her hands in excitement. "I have a great idea! What if we NEVER tell anyone we're the ones who solved the mystery even after we solve it? What if we're a secret, stealth, mystery-solving super team, and only WE know that we are? Wouldn't that be cool?"

"Yes!" agreed the other girls.

"I like the way you think, Allie," said Gina, holding her hand up for a high five. "Kind of nice and unusual."

"So, okay, I've been thinking," said Izzy, "maybe a heat

duct is blocked and it's throwing the system off."

"I found blueprints online that show the whole heating and air-conditioning system," said Allie. She opened her tablet. "See? The ducts are overhead. Heat runs through them and then comes out through vents. We'll want to start here." She pointed to a spot outside the auditorium.

"Come on," said Izzy. "Let's go check it out." The girls hurried to follow Izzy. The school seemed echoey and quiet because most students had left for the day. They reached the spot on Allie's map and looked up. They could see that branches spread out from the central duct and then ran down the halls and into the classrooms.

"The duct system is sort of like a tree," said Charlie. "It's cool!"

"It may be cool," said Marie, "but I don't understand how we're going to see if one of the ducts is blocked *inside*."

"I guess we can look into the vents," said Allie. "But we won't be able to see past the first bend in the duct. And it'll be dark, too."

"I wish we could wiggle our way through the ducts to explore them," said Gina.

"We can't," said Charlie. "We're too big to fit in the ducts."

"Thank goodness!" said Marie. "I don't want to go slithering through any heat ducts. I'm sure they're filthy inside!"

"I guess we're stumped," said Izzy.

"Maybe not," said Gina.

Everyone looked at her expectantly.

"I'm building a robot," Gina explained. "And—"

"Hold up! You're building a robot?" Allie interrupted, enchanted. "Like R2-D2?"

"Much, much simpler," said Gina. "Nothing too sci-fi, just your basic little remote-controlled vehicle."

"Could we send it through the vents?" asked Izzy.

Gina nodded. "I think so. We'd have to attach a light and a camera," she said, thinking out loud. "I know! Why don't you guys all come over to my house? I'll show you the robot I have, and we can figure out together how to adapt it. Then if we stay after school tomorrow, we can send it through the ducts."

"Um, Gina?" said Marie. "Back up a sec. If we're mucking around with the dirty vents and ducts, our clothes will get dirty."

"And your point is?" teased Charlie.

"I'll look like a mudslide!" said Marie.

"You say that as if it's a bad thing," teased Izzy.

"I was going to wear new white leggings tomorrow," moaned Marie, who always planned her week's outfits in advance. "They'll be ruined!"

Gina rolled her eyes at Marie's fussiness. "I have coveralls we can use," she said. "Don't worry. Come on."

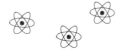

Gina's room blew them away. It was the whole top floor of the house. The room was long and narrow, and the ceiling was low, but there were big windows at either end and smaller windows that stuck out of the roof all along the sides, so there was plenty of light. There were lots of quirky nooks and crannies, too, which was a good thing, because every inch of the space was packed. Izzy almost tripped over a box of keyboards and random wires, which looked like they had come from every ancient computer in the neighborhood.

"I have a lot of projects," Gina said sort of sheepishly. She waved her hand at the stuff scattered around her room.

"All this will come in handy *some*time."

"Sure it will!" agreed Izzy, though she wasn't quite sure how any one person could have so much stuff. Gina's room looked like a mad scientist's lab.

A big, tattered poster of NASA mathematician Katherine Johnson smiled down on empty boxes of all sizes that held tools, tubes, and old computer screens. Pedals and the handlebars of a tricycle, cardboard toilet paper tubes, a stack of ancient *Popular Mechanics* magazines, a tangle of bungee cords, a jar of old buttons,

two broken manual typewriters, a music box, and four old landline telephones were crammed into various corners. Gina's bed was buried under a pile of yarn balls with knitting needles stuck in them, and a bunch of tap shoes that crowded her pillow.

"Mess drives my mom crazy," said Gina. "She insists on keeping the rest of the house neat. But as long as I 'control the chaos' as Mom says, and keep it contained up here in my room, she puts up with it."

"Where is the robot you told us about?" asked Allie.

Gina patted the head of a scruffy teddy bear encased in batteries. The bear was attached to a roller skate. "Everyone meet Teddy," Gina said. "Teddy, meet the team."

"Aww, he's so cute, Gina!" gushed Charlie.

"Well, right now he's a work in progress," said Gina, "but I can make him move with this remote control." She held up a small black box. "So if we attach a camera and lights to him, I think—"

"Whoa! Not so fast, Gina," interrupted Marie. "Where are those coveralls you said we could wear so we won't get our clothes all gunky when we work on the ducts? I'd like to put mine on now. I'm afraid if I sit down in here, I'll be covered with dust and fuzz."

"Oh," said Gina, unoffended. She scanned the room, tapping the bridge of her thick eyeglasses. "Let's see. It's kind of hard to find stuff in here."

"No kidding," said Marie.

Gina rummaged around in a box so big she nearly fell into it headfirst. Finally, she pulled out five matching coveralls with "Bob's Auto Repair" embroidered in gold thread across the back. She handed one pair of coveralls to each girl.

Charlie zipped up her coveralls. "Mine fit perfectly."

Izzy had to roll up the sleeves and pant legs, and tie a rope around her middle, but she liked her coveralls, too. Marie did not. "I hope no one sees me in this getup," she fussed as she pulled hers on. "Even if I cinch them with a belt, I look like a snowman."

"The perfect new mascot for Freezing-Cold Atom Middle School," said Izzy. "Home of the Blocked Air Ducts."

"If the ducts *are* blocked, that means that there's lots of dirt in them that'll fall out on us when we take the vent covers off and poke around inside," said Marie, frowning. "So I think we need goggles and some sort of headgear, too, to protect our eyes and heads and hair."

Gina dug to the back of her closet and found swimming goggles for everyone. Then she found a bathing cap, a construction helmet, a ski cap, a wool cap with earflaps, and a Sou'wester rain hat. The girls strapped the goggles and headgear on, and then all of them, even Marie, fell down weak with laughter when they saw in the mirror how ridiculous they looked.

"Verrrry chic," joked Izzy.

"We look like mutant creatures in a horror movie," said Charlie.

"If those guys who made your French sparkly hat got a load of these lids, they'd be green with envy," said Allie.

"*Mais OUI!*" agreed Marie in her best French accent. "*Absolument!*"

"*Now* can we get to work on the robot?" Izzy asked

eagerly, pulling off her goggles and headgear.

Gina showed the girls how she could make the teddy bear robot roll forward on its roller skate—slowly but steadily—by directing its movement with a remote. It was easy enough to attach a mini camera and small, bright lights to Teddy, but those had to be turned on and off with a separate remote. The lights had to be placed and attached

strategically so that they would illuminate the ducts but not produce so much glare that the camera's livestream would be bleached out. Meanwhile, Allie measured the robot and then clicked away on her tablet to be sure it would fit through the ducts. The girls tested the robot over and over again until Gina said they'd better stop or they'd use up the batteries.

"Well, he's not winning any robot beauty pageants, but I hope he can do the job," said Gina.

"*Shh,*" teased Charlie. She covered Teddy's ears with her hands. "You'll hurt his feelings."

Izzy put the robot on a chair. She held her fist up to Teddy's mouth, pretending that it was a microphone. "How do you feel about your journey tomorrow, Teddy? You'll be going solo, exploring the dark ducts where no one has gone before, alone in the nearly empty school. Are you ready, Teddy?"

"YES!" Marie, Gina, and Allie answered for the bear.

Charlie asked, "Where exactly are we going to have Teddy enter the duct system?"

"Good news," said Gina. "There's a safe place to take the ducts apart and send Teddy into them in our secret room near the roof. No one will see us there, and Teddy's roll-through will be all downhill since it'll start at the top of the building."

"And all uphill on the way back," sensible Charlie reminded her.

"Think Teddy's up to it?" asked Marie.

Gina shrugged. "We'll see."

11

So the next day, Thursday, after their after-school activities, the girls went up to their secret room to begin their experiment. They took off their backpacks and put on their Bob's Auto Repair coveralls over their school clothes. Then they strapped on their protective goggles and headgear.

Carefully, Gina unscrewed the bolts on either side of the thin metal band that held the ducts in place up against the ceiling. Even more carefully, she jiggled one section of the duct free and disconnected it from the rest. Less dirt and gunk shook down from the duct than Izzy had expected, but still Marie stepped back to avoid the gentle shower of dust that was dislodged.

Charlie, who was the tallest, placed Teddy in the duct.

"*Buena suerte*, Teddy," she said.

"*Bon voyage!*" said Marie, waving from the corner.

"Here goes," said Gina. "Lights, action, camera!" She powered the two remotes: one to make Teddy roll forward on his skate, and the other to turn on the lights and camera attached to him. The girls held their breath and then cheered as, with a soft whirring sound, Teddy moved forward into the duct. As soon as his fuzzy body rolled out of sight, they switched to watching Allie's laptop, on which they saw what was illuminated in front of Teddy by the lights attached to him. But Teddy had not gone very far out of sight before the girls heard a *clonk!* And the screen went dark. Gina shook the remote, checked the connections, and groaned.

"Did Teddy bump into something?" asked Izzy. "Is the duct blocked, like we thought it might be?"

"I don't know. Maybe," said Gina, furiously tapping the remote. "I can't make him move forward *or* backward."

"Poor guy!" said Charlie. "We can't leave Teddy lost and alone in there!"

"I agree," said Marie. "I know Teddy's only a robot, and machines don't have feelings, but—"

"*Shh!*" interrupted Izzy. "Listen! I think the camera's mic is picking up a sound. Hear that hum?"

All the girls were silent. Then Allie whispered, "What are we listening to?"

Charlie said, "I think Teddy has discovered a swarm of bees."

"Bees?" squeaked Allie nervously. "Do you think they're mad because Teddy bumped into them? Do you think they'll sting us?

"No," said Charlie. "When bees are swarming, they're not aggressive. They've left their hive because it's too crowded, so they don't have any brood or food to protect. Bees usually swarm in the spring, but I've seen them swarm in the fall before."

"How do you know so much about bees?" asked Gina.

"My moms keep bees," said Charlie. "And by the way, honeybees are endangered. I bet my moms would love to give those bees a home. Anybody have a big plastic bag?"

"I do!" said Gina. She reached deep into her backpack, pulled out a big trash bag, and handed the bag to Charlie. "What do you need it for?"

"I'm going to climb into the duct and get the bees," said

Charlie very matter-of-factly. "I'll get Teddy, too, of course."

"There's no way you can squeeze into that duct," said Marie. "Your shoulders are too wide."

Charlie shrugged. "Well, we'll see," she said.

"Wait!" Izzy said. Everyone looked at her. She swallowed, fighting hard against her Dizzy Izzy self, which was shaking with anxiety and fear. She plucked up her courage and thought, *Here's another chance to leave Dizzy Izzy behind.* She said, "I'll go."

Charlie said, "Izzy, you don't have to."

"I know," said Izzy. "But hey. Capturing a swarm of bees in a trash bag isn't hard compared to Forensics. It's a piece of cake! Anyway, I can fit in the ducts. So it's like sliding down the hose: It makes sense for me to do it."

"Yup, it does," said Charlie. She handed the trash bag to Izzy. "Put the bag around the swarm from the bottom up and then twist the top of the bag shut. You won't be able to get every single bee, and the ones left behind may dive-bomb and land on you. But they probably won't sting, so don't freak out. *Claro?*"

"I'll bee-eee careful," joked Izzy weakly.

Allie held her hand next to her mouth and pretended

to whisper to Marie, "Aren't you glad you were in France and missed *two whole years* of Izzy jokes?" She turned to Izzy and said, "Whatever you do, don't make any bee jokes in there. The bees'll definitely sting you if you do!"

Gina checked to be sure Izzy's headlamp worked, and then Marie, Charlie, and Allie hoisted Izzy up into the duct. Pretty soon, all that was visible of her to the other girls was the bottoms of her sneakers. Then her feet disappeared into the duct, too.

"What's it like in there?" asked Gina.

Izzy breathed out heavily and a cloud of dust poofed around her. "Just a little dusty," she said, her voice echoing in the hollow duct. "And dark." She clicked on her

headlamp and shimmied her way forward. Izzy was very grateful for her headlamp; it was darker than night inside the duct. Using her elbows to pull herself along, Izzy wiggled inch by inch farther and farther into the duct. After a while, she saw Teddy. He had become detached from his roller skate and had fallen facedown, his lights blinking forlornly, his camera askew. Izzy tucked Teddy down the back neck of her coverall and tied the roller skate to her belt. She slid her way forward like a snake. All too soon, she was right below the swarm. Warily, she opened the bag and even more warily lifted it so that the swarm was inside it. Then, as quickly as she could, she twisted the top of the bag shut and, followed by a few confused bees,

snaked in reverse, feetfirst, until she felt four sets of hands grab hold of her legs and lower her to the floor.

"Here," she said, quickly giving the bag to Charlie and then handing Teddy to Gina. She let out her breath, realizing that she had been holding it practically the whole time she was in the duct.

"You got 'em!" said Charlie. "Way to go, Izzy."

"Great," squeaked Allie, sounding a bit undone at the sight of a big, buzzing bag of bees.

"I'd better bring these bees home right away," said Charlie. "They'll be happy to be let out of the bag, and my moms will be really happy to get a whole new colony."

"We'd better postpone examining the ducts till another day," said Allie.

"Want to come home with me and see my moms release the bees?" asked Charlie.

"Okay!" said the other girls.

Izzy rode her bike straight to Charlie's house without stopping to take off her coverall or headlamp. She forgot! She was thinking too hard about what she and her friends should try next.

"So should we fix Teddy and try again?" asked Gina. It was the next morning, and the girls were in their secret room, before their morning classes.

"No," said Izzy. "Just past where the bees were, the ducts divide into branches that are too narrow even for Teddy to squeeze through."

"What do you do if you *can't* conduct the experiment that you want to conduct?" asked Charlie.

Izzy opened the composition book. "I guess you just put that hypothesis aside," she said. "In this case, on ice," she said. She wrote in the book:

- Make an Observation: The school is too cold.
- Form a Question: Why is the air-conditioning/ heating system malfunctioning?
- Form a Hypothesis: A heat duct is blocked.
- Conduct an Experiment: Send robot Teddy through the heat ducts to look for blockage.
- Analyze the Data and Draw a Conclusion: Ducts too narrow. Unable to collect data. Unable to draw a conclusion.

Marie looked over Izzy's shoulder. "You should write: Ducts were a dead end," she said.

"It kind of seems like *all* our ideas are dead ends so far," said Allie.

"Maybe we should all just resign ourselves to freezing," said Gina. "Because I'll admit, I'm racking my brain, but I'm at a dead end when it comes to coming up with new hypotheses."

"*¡Ajá!* And I'll admit, I'm just plain tired of dead ends," said Charlie.

"And I'm just plain dead tired of trying," said Marie.

They all looked at Izzy. "Uh-oh," said Charlie. "Izzy's got that dangerous 'I've got an idea' look on her face again."

Izzy laughed, but she meant it when she said, "We can't give up *now*. I've got lots more hypotheses we can test."

"Like what?" asked Allie.

"Like, is the air-conditioning or heating system on a clock or a timer that's malfunctioning?" said Izzy. "Or is the air-conditioning's electronic system connected by mistake to some other system—say, the fire alarm or burglar alarm—so it is responding to a false 'On' signal?

Or has a fuse blown? Or—"

"You've convinced us," Charlie interrupted. She smiled with affection at her friend. "Izzy, talk about 'On' signals! *Your* 'On' signal is *stuck* on."

Izzy grinned. "I'm sure the rest of you will think of some new things to try, too," she said.

She led the way down the stairs and through the auditorium into the hallway. The rest of the girls followed her. Suddenly, all of them came to a halt. Because smack in front of the principal's office, where there were still orange traffic cones to keep kids away from the jumble of the scaffolding and repair equipment, someone had changed the sign that usually said ATOM MIDDLE SCHOOL so that it now read WHATOMESS MIDDLE SCHOOL.

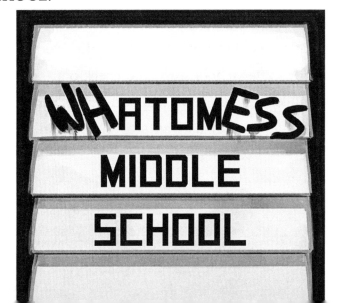

"Yikes," said Izzy. "Guess the crowd is getting restless."

Charlie nodded. "We really, *really* better solve the Mystery of the Cold School, or there will be a revolution."

"Well, Allie and I know where the fuse box is," said Gina. "Our blueprints show that it's near the gym, in a utility room. Do you want to check out your hypotheses about blown fuses or the air-conditioning system being connected to a timer or the fire alarm, Izzy? We could go at lunch."

"I have a Pep Squad power lunch today," said Allie. "So you guys go without me."

"Nope," said Izzy. "We'll all go. We're a squad, too."

"Right—we're the Smart Squad," said Charlie, smiling at her own cleverness.

"Gina and I can stay after school today," said Marie. "My sister has the day off from work, so we don't have to babysit Crosby. Let's meet at the utility room after everybody's after-school stuff, and check out the fuses." She grinned. "I guess Izzy's stubbornness is contagious. It looks like *none* of us wants to give up on solving this case!"

12

Once again, Izzy's hypothesis proved wrong.

That afternoon, when the girls examined the fuse boxes and electrical circuits, they saw that there was no timer or alarm connected to the air-conditioning or heating systems.

"And none of the fuses are blown," said Izzy, "so that means that this hypothesis *is* blown."

The girls trudged upstairs to their secret room near the roof. They were all too discouraged to talk. Even Izzy's stream of ideas had run dry. Marie sat down and began leafing through the composition book in which Izzy had kept their notes. It was a bit tattered now. There were watermarks on the front cover, and some of the pages were stuck together with ketchup streaks.

"None of the hypotheses in that book worked," sighed Charlie, watching Marie.

"What'll we do now?" asked Allie. "Give up on solving the cold problem and build campfires in the classrooms?"

"Bring in heat lamps?" joked Gina. "Wear long underwear?"

"Long underwear is a fashion don't," dismissed Marie, only half-joking.

Izzy slid down onto the floor next to Marie and looked at the book with her.

As Marie flipped back to the first page in the book, Allie asked, "We should just toss that thing. We don't need *old* ideas; we need *new* ones."

"Well," said Izzy, "our old ideas are new ideas to Marie and Gina."

"Right," said Marie. "Like, what was your first hypothesis? Where did you start?"

"We started with the thermostat," said Izzy, pointing to the first page in the book. "It's in Mr. Delmonico's office. We thought that maybe because it's in direct sunlight, it registered a high temperature and kept kicking the air-conditioning *on* and turning the furnace *off*."

"Oh, yeah," said Marie. "I saw the thermostat when Gina and I met with the principal to ask about the lights on the stairs."

"Speaking of lights," said Gina. "I've invented a way to remind us NOT to let the door slam shut behind us so no one will ever be trapped on the roof again." She took a little gizmo out of her backpack. "See this LED light bulb? I've made a circuit that connects it to the door. It's wired so that the light bulb will blink on and off until you throw the bolt to stop the door from shutting all the way."

"Thanks," said Charlie. "You're a genius, Gina. We should replace all the old bulbs in this room with LED bulbs. They don't get so hot, and they last longer so they're better for the environment."

"Well, I just happen to have an extra LED bulb," said Gina. She held it out to Charlie. "Here."

Suddenly, Izzy yelped. She jumped up and bounced on her toes.

"Izzy?" said Charlie. "Are you okay?"

Izzy nodded. She was so excited that she stumbled over her words. "I think, I mean, oh, what if?" Finally, she gave up trying to explain, took the LED light bulb from Charlie, and gestured to her friends, saying, "Come with me!"

Izzy led a small stampede through the halls. When the girls got to the principal's office, Izzy screeched to a stop. She signaled for the girls to cram into a doorway with her.

"What is going on?" hissed Marie.

"*Shh,*" Izzy shushed. "Mr. Delmonico is in there."

"Duh," said Allie. "Hello? It's his *office.*"

"We have to get him out of there," said Izzy.

"Why?" asked Gina.

"How?" asked Marie.

"What for?" asked Allie.

Charlie didn't ask any questions. She said, "It'll look fishy if we call him out here for no reason, Izzy."

"Then we'll just have to go into his office and distract him," said Izzy.

"Okay," said Charlie, "but you're going to have to do the distracting. You're the only one who has a good excuse to talk to Mr. Delmonico. Ask him if he's read your STEM team proposal."

Izzy entire body clenched, head to toe. "Can't one of you talk to him?" she begged.

"No!" said Allie, Charlie, Marie, and Gina all together.

"How'll I get him away from his desk?" asked Izzy.

"You'll think of something," said Charlie.

"We'll be right behind you," said Marie.

"I'm not budging until someone tells me what's going on," said Allie, stamping her foot.

So Izzy explained. "I think the air-conditioning keeps going *on* and the furnace keeps going *off* because Mr. Delmonico put a desk lamp with an old-fashioned light bulb right under the thermostat. The thermostat registers a high temperature as if the whole building is hot," she said. She held up Gina's bulb. "This LED bulb won't generate as much heat, so it won't fool the thermostat. We're going to switch bulbs."

"Well, it's worth a try," said Gina. She took the LED bulb from Izzy and said, "You talk. I'll switch." She grinned and held the bulb above Izzy's head, joking, "It's your bright idea, after all!"

"Okay," said Izzy. "Let's go." She took a deep breath and knocked on Mr. Delmonico's door. Allie, Gina, Marie, and Charlie were packed tightly behind her and so abuzz with nerves that Izzy felt like they were a bee swarm.

Mr. Delmonico looked up. "Come in, girls," he said. "What can I do for you?"

Everyone waited for Izzy to speak. But Izzy was petrified: She was so scared stiff that she felt as if she had been turned to stone. It was like Forensics multiplied by stage fright with a scoop of shyness on top, only worse. Allie gave her a little shove forward, but Izzy could not make her mouth work.

Allie came to her rescue. "This is Izzy Newton," she said. "The girl who suggested a STEM team."

"Oh, yes!" said Mr. Delmonico. "Izzy, I gave your proposal to the board for their consideration. Good research work, by the way."

"Mxntks," Izzy croaked. After that failed attempt at saying thanks, she couldn't think of anything else to say.

Charlie spoke up. "We were thinking that the board might ask you what kind of project a STEM team could do for the school. And, uh, for example, look out this window."

When Mr. Delmonico got up from his desk and went to the window, Gina unscrewed the light bulb from his lamp. The bulb was hot, so she pulled her sleeve down over her hand to protect it.

"Yes?" asked Mr. Delmonico.

Charlie had a desperate look on her face. Izzy could tell that she was stuck. Marie took over. "Look up at the roof above the auditorium," she said. "A STEM team could plant grass up there and make this building a green school."

"Well," said Mr. Delmonico. He started to turn away from the window, but Izzy pointed and redirected his attention. Her voice sounded strangled because she was so nervous, but she managed to say, "And maybe we could put wind turbines up there to generate our own electricity."

"Well," said Mr. Delmonico again. "I—"

"Green buildings save money," said Gina. She appeared at Izzy's elbow, so Izzy knew she'd switched the bulbs.

Mission accomplished, thought Izzy, weak with relief.

"Well," said Mr. Delmonico a third time. "I—"

"That's all we wanted to say," said Marie abruptly. She turned toward the door. "So, thanks! Bye!"

Mr. Delmonico looked a little surprised as the girls made a hasty retreat, stumbling over one another in their hurry to get out of the principal's office. "Thanks, Mr. Delmonico! Bye!" they echoed Marie. "Bye!"

Mr. Delmon

Once outside the office, the girls collapsed. "Nice job, everybody," said Izzy. "You guys are The Best. I never want to do anything like that in my life ever again!"

"Not to be a downer," said Allie as the girls left school, "but I don't think you should get your hopes up about this latest hypothesis, Izzy. The bulb is such an easy solution. How come none of the technicians thought of it?"

"How come it took *us* so long to think of it?" added Charlie. "It's so simple."

"Yup. It's an example of Occam's razor," Izzy said as she nodded cheerfully.

"Whose what?" asked Gina.

"This guy Occam that Granddad told me about," said Izzy. "His rule is that 'simplest is best.' You shouldn't assume something is more complicated than it appears." She grinned at her friends. "I guess by lunchtime Monday, we'll know if old Occam's as sharp as his razor."

Once again, Izzy was wrong.

It didn't take until lunchtime. By mid-morning Monday, it was clear that the air-conditioning was off and staying off. At long last, the school building was a comfortable temperature. Students cheered as they shed the heavy outer clothing they'd been wearing to stay warm inside the school. They kicked off their thick boots and spun their coats above their heads in celebration. The air was full of mittens tossed like very bulky celebratory confetti.

Izzy, Allie, Charlie, Gina, and Marie stood together in the hall and watched as a bunch of eighth graders danced down the hall, fanning themselves with their notebooks while chatting and laughing.

Then Mr. Delmonico came on the PA system and made an announcement. "Students of Atom Middle School," he said, "I am happy to declare our deep freeze is over. With the help of the skilled air-conditioning technicians, I have solved the problem and the school is now a comfortable temperature."

"Hooray!" cheered all the students in the halls and all the classrooms. "Way to go, Mr. Delmonico!"

Izzy, Allie, Charlie, Marie, and Gina raised their

eyebrows at one another and exchanged secret smiles. Without saying a word, Izzy held the composition book open so that Allie, Charlie, Marie, and Gina could see it. She had written:

- Make an Observation: The school is too cold.
- Form a Question: Why is the air-conditioning/ heating system malfunctioning?
- Form a Hypothesis: An old-fashioned light bulb right under the thermostat makes it register a high temperature.
- Conduct an Experiment: Replace the old-fashioned light bulb with an LED bulb.

- Analyze the Data and Draw a Conclusion: After installation, it is clear that the LED bulb solved the problem.

"We know who *really* solved the problem," said Marie. "It was you, Izzy. You're the absolute hero."

"Oh, no," said Izzy. "There's no *one* absolute hero. It was all of us working together. Anyway," she said modestly, "our solution was just common sense."

"I don't think so," said Allie, who was never reluctant to boast. "I think our solution was brilliant. We are some seriously smart girls."

After school, the girls went up to the roof. Thanks to Gina's blinking light, they remembered to slide the bolt so the door wouldn't lock behind them. They tilted their faces up to the sun and took deep breaths of the fall air that was fragrant with the aroma of leaves.

"I love how we have a three-hundred-and-sixty degree view from this roof," said Allie, turning slowly to take it all in.

"Oh, we are going to have big fun up here," Gina sighed contentedly. "Izzy, want to build a wind turbine together?"

"Yes," said Izzy. "And when I earn enough money for a telescope, we can have a sleepover and stay awake looking at the stars; wouldn't that be"—she grinned—"out of this world?"

"Cosmic," Allie added, smiling at the space-related puns.

"Before the ground freezes, we can clear the weeds out of those old boxes," said Charlie. "I've already collected seedlings to plant. In the spring, we'll have a vegetable garden. There's nothing more delicious than homegrown strawberries." She smiled. "I'm even hoping that I can talk you guys into having our own beehive. Think of the honey!"

"It sure is already great up here," said Marie. "And we'll make it even *better.*" She smiled at Izzy, Allie, and Charlie. "I don't think I ever thanked you three for telling Gina and me about the secret room and the roof. Thanks!"

"And thanks for letting us be part of your squad of smart girls," said Gina.

"That's the five of us," said Allie. "You, me, Marie, Charlie, and Izzy. We're the smart squad."

"S-M-A-R-T," said Marie. "That stands for Solving Mysteries—"

"And Revealing Truths!" finished Izzy, smiling at Marie, her wonderful, lost-then-found friend. "We are The Best."

"I hope we'll have lots more mysteries to solve," said Charlie. "And if we do, let's keep on keeping our mystery-solving a secret. It'll be cooler if we are the only ones who know, right?"

"Right!" all the girls agreed.

"I wonder what our *next* S.M.A.R.T. Squad challenge will be?" said Gina.

"Who knows?" said Izzy. "But whatever it is, we'll solve it together."

THE TRUTH BEHIND THE FICTION

Who's Who? And Which One Are You?

The S.M.A.R.T. Squad characters are all modeled after famous scientists, each of whom studied a different subject or field. Take a look at these world-renowned thinkers, and you will see how each character got her name. You may also notice that it's not just their names that are similar but some of their interests, too. Which field of interest interests YOU?

SIR ISAAC NEWTON

Born: January 4, 1643

Fields of Interest: Physics: light, heat, sound, motion, and force

BFF: John Wickins (Recognize the name of Izzy's cat?)

Hobbies: Flute, stargazing, color theory, alchemy (That's trying to make gold.)

Claim to Fame: Newton explained the theory of universal gravity, discovered the branch of mathematics called calculus, and developed three laws of motion that pretty much underlie all the basic principles of modern physics:

1. Objects in motion stay in motion and objects at rest stay at rest unless acted upon by a force.
2. Acceleration depends on force and mass.
3. For every action, there is an equal and opposite reaction.

CHARLES DARWIN

Born: February 12, 1809

Fields of Interest: Biology and botany, which includes the study of plants, fish, bugs, and lots more

BFFs: T. H. Huxley, a biologist who studied birds and dinosaurs; Charles Lyell, a geologist who explained how Earth changed over time; and Darwin's wife, Emma, and their children

Hobbies: Collecting plants and animals; definitely NOT sailing. He would get violently seasick while on his voyage of discovery.

Claim to Fame: Darwin sailed around the world for nearly five years on a ship called the *Beagle* and wrote *On the Origin of Species by Means of Natural Selection,* a book that revolutionized science by showing that plants and animals are constantly changing or "evolving."

GEORGE WASHINGTON CARVER

Born: Approximately 1864

Fields of Interest: Plants, animals—anything that grows!

BFF: Booker T. Washington

Hobbies: Painting, breaking barriers: Carver was the first African American to attend what would become Tuskegee University. He later became the school's first African-American faculty member.

Claim to Fame: Carver invented and/or promoted non-food uses for peanuts, sweet potatoes, cowpeas, alfalfa, wild plums, tomatoes, and corn. He wrote about better ways of growing crops; raising poultry, cows, and hogs; preserving meats in hot weather; and the importance of including nature study in schools.

MARIE CURIE

Born: November 7, 1867

Fields of Interest: Chemistry, physics, and math

BFFS: Her husband, Pierre, and daughters, Irène and Ève

Hobbies: Bike riding

Claim to Fame: Not only was Curie the first woman to win a Nobel Prize, she is the only woman to win two Nobel Prizes and she was awarded them for two different fields (physics and chemistry). Curie researched radioactivity and techniques for isolating radioactive isotopes. She discovered two elements, polonium and radium.

ALBERT EINSTEIN

Born: March 14, 1879 (That's 3.14—Pi Day!)

Fields of Interest: Chemistry, physics, math, space, time—you name it!

BFFS: His sister, Maja

Hobbies: Playing the violin, sailing, hiking

Claim to Fame: Einstein developed the theory of relativity, which states that time is relative to motion, nothing moves faster than light, and the gravity of huge bodies like the sun can bend space-time. (Think of a beam of starlight curving as it passes near the sun). Einstein wrote the world's most famous equation, $E = mc^2$: energy equals mass times the speed of light squared. This equation essentially means that energy and mass are different forms of the same thing! Einstein also won the Nobel Prize in Physics.

WOMEN SCIENTISTS

You know the S.M.A.R.T. Squad is super brainy, but do you know about these amazing real-life female scientists? Some of their work helped change the world; others are working on experiments today that could have an impact on our future.

KATHERINE JOHNSON: SPACE PIONEER

Born in West Virginia in 1918, Katherine Johnson was a math and physics genius who used her extraordinary ability for complicated calculations to figure out not only how to launch crewed spacecraft but also their best trajectories and return paths. Part of nearly every space mission team up to 1986, Johnson calculated where and when spacecraft would land after orbiting Earth. Johnson computed a path for Apollo 11 to get to the moon—and back; she calculated how the lunar module could reconnect with the command module in order to return home safely. Johnson was essential to the beginning of the space shuttle program and worked on plans for a mission to Mars. In 2015, President Barack Obama awarded Johnson the Presidential Medal of Freedom.

Katherine Johnson at NASA Research Center

GRACE HOPPER: COMPUTER SCIENTIST

Born in New York City in 1906, Grace Hopper was brilliant, determined, and way ahead of her time. She was one of the very first computer scientists back in 1944, when computers were as big as a whole room. Hopper was also a rear admiral in the United States Navy. She was a pioneer programmer on an early computer called the Mark I. You should thank her every day because she invented one of the first "linkers," or languages that enabled computers and people to communicate.

Grace Hopper codes onto punch tape for a new calculating machine.

186

These two National Geographic explorers are among many scientists at work today whose studies will help our planet.

LINA ARAGÓN: BIOLOGIST AND PLANT ECOLOGIST

Aragón in Colombia at a unique alpine ecosystem in the tropics

Lina Aragón is a graduate school student, working on her PhD in ecology and environmental biology at the University of Waterloo in Canada. As a biologist, Aragón is passionate about plant botany, physiology, and ecology. She is especially fascinated in the way plants thrive under unbelievably extreme conditions around the world. She is interested in applying this knowledge to better understand how plants will respond to climate change and how our planet will change as a consequence of this phenomenon.

ANTONELLA WILBY: ROBOTICS ENGINEER AND COMPUTER SCIENTIST

Antonella Wilby is a robotics engineer, conservation technologist, and underwater explorer who builds robots to explore extreme environments. She develops cutting-edge robotics and technology to help understand ocean ecosystems, study endangered species, and map unexplored environments, with the goal of better understanding and protecting our planet. Currently, her research focuses on building a swarm of robots to create detailed three-dimensional maps of coral reefs to help ecologists better understand coral reef ecosystems. As part of this work, she develops software that enables robots to "see" with their cameras, enabling them to autonomously navigate, build 3D maps, and understand the complex underwater world around them.

Wilby deploys the SphereCam in the Gulf of California, Mexico.

187

S.M.A.R.T. TERMINOLOGY

The S.M.A.R.T. Squad talks about all kinds of scientific and mathematical concepts. But what's behind these complex ideas? Let's take a closer look.

Absolute Zero

In the story, Izzy feels like an absolute zero when Marie is cold to her. Absolute zero is the lowest possible temperature. Theoretically, nothing could be colder. At absolute zero, particles have minimal vibrational motion and, therefore, no heat. It is zero on the kelvin scale, equivalent to minus 273.15°C or minus 459.67°F. Brrr!

The Scientific Method

Remember the notebook Izzy kept to record all the ways the S.M.A.R.T. Squad tried to solve the Mystery of the Cold School? Izzy applied the scientific method, which is a series of steps that scientists follow, to answer questions. Use it yourself on a question that's bugging you, like this:

Make an Observation: I am so hungry by 9:30 a.m. that I could eat my math book.

Form a Question: Does what I eat for breakfast make a difference?

Form a Hypothesis: If I eat protein, like eggs, for breakfast, I'll be fuller longer.

Conduct an Experiment: Week One: Eat eggs for breakfast Monday through Friday; note time hunger sets in. Week Two: Eat cereal for breakfast Monday through Friday; note time hunger sets in.

Analyze the Data and Draw a Conclusion: Both weeks, stomach growled by 9:30 a.m. Protein for breakfast made no difference. Pack a snack!

Occam's Razor

Occam's razor is a rule of logic that's behind all scientific modeling and theory development. Simply put, it says don't make more assumptions than you need to. In the story, Izzy's grandfather tells her about Occam's razor when she is guessing why Marie cut off their friendship. Later, Izzy applies Occam's razor to the Mystery of the Cold School. The solution was simple: Apply Occam's razor to a problem you've made more complicated than it needs to be, like:

My dog keeps whimpering and whining. Is he sick? Does he hear/smell/feel an earthquake coming? Is he hungry again? (I just fed him an hour ago!) Has he injured his paw? Is my brother calling him from outside? Is he frightened by the music I'm playing? Has he lost his chew toy? Does he want me to pet him? Is he just being a needy pain in the neck? Oh. He needs to go out. Sorry, fella.

LED

LED stands for light-emitting diode. LED bulbs last a long time; if you used one for 8 hours a day, by some estimates it would last for 17 years, which is approximately 50 times longer than a typical incandescent bulb. LED bulbs require much less wattage than incandescent light bulbs, which is why LEDs are more energy efficient and last longer. Crucial to Izzy and the S.M.A.R.T. Squad in solving their mystery is the fact that LED bulbs do not feel hot. They keep their cool.

IZZY NEWTON AND THE S.M.A.R.T. SQUAD

NEWTON'S FLAW

Izzy cleared her throat. It felt a little tight and itchy, maybe from the uncomfortable feeling that headstrong Allie was wrong to just breezily assume that Marie would like her science fair project without even asking her. Izzy met Charlie's glance; they both knew that Marie and Allie were impatient with one another sometimes. Allie drove Marie crazy with her "the more the merrier" full-speed-ahead enthusiasm and bossiness. And Marie drove Allie crazy with how fussy and finicky she could be. Izzy swallowed hard, not knowing what to say, not wanting to make the hairline fracture between Allie and Marie bigger.

Fortunately, at that moment, Allie made a whopper sneeze. "Ahh-choo!"

Ms. Okeke, the librarian, came over to their table. "Hello, girls," she said. Her voice sounded nasal because she had a stuffy nose. She handed Allie a box of tissues. "Help yourself to a tissue."

"Thanks," said Allie. She dabbed her red-rimmed eyes and blew her nose.

Ms. Okeke sighed, but it turned into a cough. "I'm sniffly, too," she rasped. "Lately, it seems like everyone who comes to the library is attacked by upper respiratory congestion."

Izzy sat up straight and listened carefully. She sensed a mystery!

"Now that you mention it, my eyes and nose have been runny ever since I came in here this afternoon," said Gina.

"My throat is itchy," said Izzy hoarsely.

"I have sort of a headache," Charlie admitted.

Allie didn't say anything, but she blew her nose with a loud honk.

"What is going on?" asked Charlie. "What's giving everyone these weird symptoms?"

"It's a puzzle," said Ms. Okeke, "and if someone could solve it, I'd be grateful."

Ms. Okeke left, and Gina, Izzy, and Charlie exchanged excited, delighted grins.

"Are you thinking what I'm thinking?" asked Izzy. She rhymed the syllables, "The Li-brar-ee Mys-ter-ee. Has a nice ring to it, right? Sure does sound like a job for the S.M.A.R.T. Squad."

ACKNOWLEDGMENTS:

One hot September Saturday, my friend Carolyn Johnson emailed me and asked if by any chance, I could be a last-minute substitute speaker at a luncheon for librarians she was hosting that Wednesday. I said, "Sure!" I'll do anything for Carolyn: She's the kind of librarian friend who suggests books for you to read and you read them and LOVE them. I had a wonderful time at the luncheon, where I met a very nice young woman named Becky Baines. A month went by, and then Becky Baines emailed me and wrote that she was the executive editor at Nat Geo Kids Books. Would I be interested in writing a fiction series?

Would I? I thought it would only be a total dream come true!

And I was right. Working with Becky and Kate Hale and Erica Green on Izzy's stories has been fantastic. I'm also grateful to book designer Julide Dengel, photo editor Sarah Mock, and production editor Molly Reid. When the sketches came in from Geneva Bowers, I was thrilled. Geneva brought Izzy and her friends to life. Her illustrations expressed the whimsical, joyful spirit of Izzy's stories perfectly, just perfectly. I am grateful to Geneva and everyone at National Geographic Kids: They're a grown-up S.M.A.R.T. Squad. And thank you, Carolyn, for inviting me to that luncheon!

Stories must be authentic, so before I began writing I met with my thoughtful and articulate friend Maggie Welsh, a student at Silver Spring International Middle School, who told me what middle school is like right now, today, for students like her. Maggie helped me get my stories off on the right foot. My dear friend Anne Sprout arranged for me to speak to a lovely, lively group of sixth-grade girls at the school where she is the librarian. We had a blast. I couldn't scribble fast enough to capture all the great ideas the girls had, popping like popcorn! And talk about fun: My bright, beguiling Lunch Bunch girls at St. John the Evangelist School in Silver Spring, Maryland, inspired, encouraged, informed, and delighted me every time we met. I'd bring animal crackers and questions, and they'd bring enthusiasm, insights, and answers. I am forever grateful to their teacher, Maureen Rossi. And oh, I can never thank you enough my Lunch Bunch girls—Arsema, Kika, Nora, Madelyn, Baeza, Caroline, Emily, and Colleen—but here's a start: THANK YOU!

—*Valerie Tripp*